THE HAPPY SQUIRE:
Christmas
STORIES TO ENCOURAGE & INSPIRE

The real reason the three Wise Men gave gold, frankincense, and myrrh instead of actual baby gifts (and why men were banned from baby showers).

Written (& illustrations) by Chad David
www.ChadDavid.ca

Forward by Rita Carrey
www.PeetandReet.com

Cover art by Aidan Hennebry
www.hushhushphotofilm.com

Dedications

Rita: The Forward of this book is dedicated to my older brother, John, who passed away in 2019 after a long fight with leukemia. He was a fabulous worker, provider, father, and husband who loved music and anything with an engine. I will miss him greatly, but find solace that he is at peace.

Chad: This book is dedicated to my sister and brother, Lori and Eric – two people who helped me become a sap for Christmas.

Table of Contents

8

If you have an <u>idea</u> for a Christmas story or an inspiring Christmas <u>memory</u> or <u>tradition</u> you'd like considered being included in a future book, please submit to Chad's website:

www.ChadDavid.ca.

Author's Note: I have a little sign that I put up every Christmas that says, "Leave every place a little merrier than when you found it." Rita lives this statement. Despite going through some incredible trials and losses, she has always gotten back up and continues to bring joy everywhere she goes. Her exuberance and joyful spirit make life feel better when she's around. It's as if she lives with the Christmas spirit (on maple syrup overload) all year round. It is such a privilege to have her contribute a few stories and thoughts to my book, especially because if anyone represents the spirit of Christmas, it's her.

Christmas Thoughts & Memories:
A Forward by Rita Carrey

I learned that Christmas is a time for magic from the best. I remember when I was really young, my parents had John, Jim (my two brothers), and I sleep in the same room Christmas Eve in order to share in our excitement about Christmas Day. After saying good-night to our parents and closing the door to our room, we soon heard what sounded like jingling sleigh-bells. We immediately ran to our parents who were casually sitting with each other on the couch, and we asked them about the sleigh-bells. My mom said she was surprised that we heard bells as if to say she hadn't heard anything, but then she added, "If you heard sleigh-bells, you better get to sleep because that means Santa is close." Talk about a command we couldn't follow – get to sleep? No way! But we quickly ran back to our room as we were told; after all, Santa was watching and we didn't want to screw things up this close to Christmas. Getting to our room, we jumped into our beds, which is when we heard the bells again. This time my brothers and I got up and ran to the window to see if we could spot Santa... and we did! We saw a red light in the distance – whoa – and as we stared in amazement at the light, we heard more sleigh-bells jingling. It really was him! As a five-year-old, it didn't get better than that. We'd stay up feeding off of each others' imaginations as we created an excited hysteria. When we eventually got to bed, we continued to hear sleigh-bells jingling off and on throughout the night. It was all so magical.

When we were older, I found out that after my brothers and I were in our bedroom, my mom was sneaking around jingling sleigh-bells to sound like Santa, which I thought was great in its own way because she purposely helped us have a magical experience. And she wasn't done there. Earlier in the day when we were distracted, she went into our room and strapped sleigh-bells to the bottom of our beds, so even when she wasn't jingling the bells herself, we could still hear them off and on throughout the night as we moved around in our beds. The one thing that I'm still not sure about is if the light in the distance was part of her plan like she wanted us in that specific room because the view from our window included hydro lines and that, to an excited five-year-old's imagination, looked like Santa in the distance. Either way, my parents knew how to make Christmas special, and this bell jingling became a tradition that continued throughout our childhood and even for our own kids.

One of the most exciting moments of the Christmas season was the day the Eaton's catalogue arrived in the mail. Those are two words you don't hear very often anymore: (20 year old) "What is an Eat-on? Is that like a futon table? And is a cat-a-log like a disturbing French cheese log made of cat's milk?" The arrival of the catalogue marked the official start of Christmas dreaming – yea! My brothers and I would spend hours carefully comparing each others' ideas and choosing the one big gift we'd ask for from Santa. We'd also be able to pick out a few smaller things to give ideas to my parents and relatives, but it was really all about that one big present. Back then, that was what dreams were made of for kids like us. It's amazing how things change.

What hasn't changed, like most kids, I would enjoy sneaking around trying to find any presents I could before Christmas morning, but I never found any... not that I really wanted to. It just added to the excitement. I later found out my mom had our neighbors, a very kind elderly couple, hold onto all the gifts for her, so my brothers and I would never be able to spoil the surprise of what we were getting. She was always a step ahead.

The one thing Mom and Dad taught us about Santa that other parents often miss was that he never wrapped his presents. He was a toymaker, which meant he would leave his gift all assembled and ready to be played with as soon as it was found under the tree Christmas morning. This really added to the excitement as my brothers and I would wake up and find things like a racecar set all ready to go. There were always a few wrapped presents from relatives under the tree and there was even a wrapped gift from Rudolph, but they really just accented the main gifts – the big ones from Santa my brothers and I had been anxiously looking forward to since choosing them from the catalogue from what felt like years before. They were by far the highlight of the tree and Christmas morning (I'm sure God will forgive me for thinking that).

One Christmas Eve, as always, my brothers and I were too excited to sleep. This year, however, for some reason we got up and went to see our parents in the living room. Unlike the previous time when my mom expected to see us, when we got to the room, we were surprised to find a half made go kart beside the Christmas tree. On the one hand, it was exciting, "A go kart!" but at the same time, "Why is it only half a go kart?" My brother, the one who had asked for it, started to cry. Was Santa mad at him? Did Santa not love him as much? Was he one mistake away from being on the Naughty List, so he only got part of the gift? Fortunately, my mom was as cool as ever as she calmly said, "This is why you don't leave your room Christmas Eve. You have to go back to sleep, so Santa will return and finish the rest." In the morning, as promised, the go kart was in one piece – Santa had been there... twice! My mom had been able to turn a sad moment into a very special experience. She was the perfect blend of clever and pleasantly devious.

And where was my dad in all of this? He was on the apartment balcony with instructions and pieces to half of a go kart trying to hide from the kids who got up when they weren't supposed to. He was the magic behind the scenes supporting my mom to help make Christmas wonderful. Together, they were an unstoppable team.

One of my favourite Christmas memories best demonstrates my mom's sneaky genius. One Christmas, my brothers and I wanted to do something special for Santa. Everyone gave milk, so that was boring. We wanted to stand out. We decided to tell Mom we wanted to leave Santa cookies (because cookies are never boring) *and* a can of pop. Cans were a new thing at the time (I'm younger than that makes me sound), and this was our way of showing how much we appreciated him. My mom "tried" to convince us that a can was a bad idea because Santa had a beard. That meant it would be hard for him to drink from it, but we didn't care what she said. We *had* to give him a can of pop.

When we got up Christmas morning, and after getting up Mom and Dad (the one strict rule we had to follow) we ran to see if Santa received the gift we left him. As we had hoped, the cookie plate only had a few crumbs left on it and beside it was an empty pop can, but... the empty pop can wasn't completely empty. The pop was gone, but there... inside the can... was white beard hair. Whooooaaaaa... we had a piece of Santa's beard! That was the one gift better than anything the Eaton's catalogue offered. Mom was right. Drinking from a can was hard for Santa, and it must have snagged off a piece of his beard. Our pop idea was more genius than we could've imagined. As we stared in amazement at the tuft of hair, my mom said we should put it in the freezer. When we asked why, she said, "Well, Santa comes from the North Pole, so if you don't put it in the freezer, it's going to melt and disappear." As kids, this logic made complete sense (even though it doesn't). I can't remember how long we kept the hair in the freezer, but we were very proud of ourselves. No one else had this. We were the only ones we knew to actually have real proof of Santa.

As you can probably guess, my brothers and I believed in Santa a lot longer than the average child... and it was wonderful because it added to the excitement of Christmas.

Years later we found out that Mom had bought angel hair to use as Santa's beard and then planted the idea in our heads to leave Santa a can of pop. She was that good that she made us think it was our idea to leave out a pop can because she had this plan to help make that Christmas morning one of the most special moments in my childhood.

It didn't matter what time of year it was, my mom had a knack for surprises and making things special. For instance, the one day my brothers came home from school, they discovered she had redecorated their bedroom... and not in a normal way. She had made hanging lamps and a few other decorations she put up and placed their mini pool table in the middle of the room to turn it into a pool hall. It was pretty great. For me, when I was eight, I came home from school to find... she had fun. She separated and spread out my bunk bed, put out some throw pillows, put up daisy wallpaper, and moved a TV into my room to make it look more like a cool living room. My friends were really impressed. The craziest thing is she used dye and Javex to make a giant swirly pattern in the carpet. Who tie-dyes a rug? I'd be too scared of doing it wrong, but not her. She was fearless when it came to decorating because she loved to freak you out and she was good at it. Over the years she had repainted everything in our apartment. And I mean everything. She had even repainted the couch – the couch! She had found a special material paint, so why not? Probably the craziest thing she painted was my dad's car – not professionally. She used a roller. That's right – a standard wall-painting roller! It's safe to say her goal of freaking people out was achieved with that one. When it came to my mom, my dad was a very understanding man... to put it mildly.

What's interesting is we had the rich cousins who lived in a swanky house near us in Toronto while we were the poor side of the family who lived in an apartment. Whenever my brothers and I visited our cousins, their parents gave us money to go out to dinner at a restaurant. We thought that was the best thing in the world because we never got to do that. Meanwhile, when our cousins came to our apartment, my mom made us dinner and we ate together as a family and my cousins thought that was the best thing in the world because they never got to do that. It's amazing how perspective really affects you. Being poor was one of the reasons why my mom's ability to make things so special was all the more impressive. She had to be very creative to do what she did. Together, my parents worked at using what they had to give us the best possible childhood they could, and it ended up being one that was full of fantastic memories.

One of my favourite traditions growing up happened Friday night; if we were good we were allowed to watch the late night movie channel to see a scary movie. My mom's rule was if you're going to be scared, you can't watch it. We all wanted to see the movies, so even if we were scared, we never said anything. Our love of scary things was why the original *A Christmas Carol* was one of the movies we had to watch every year. As a kid (and for some adults), this version of Scrooge was scary, which made it all the better. Our other go-to movie was *The Grinch*, which was more about how he became good in the end. Movies like *It's a Wonderful Life* were fun, but it wasn't Christmas if we didn't get to watch *A Christmas Carol* and *The Grinch* (funny how life works out).

Author's Note: As much as I love Rita, I have to disagree with her; the best version of the Scrooge story is *The Muppet Christmas Carol*. That might just show how much more manly I am, but the Christmas Carol story isn't the same without Gonzo and Rizzo narrating it and there being a singing Tiny Tim who fills your heart with warmth while crushing it with sadness at the same time. Manly men know what I mean.

One of my biggest Christmas surprises wasn't actually planned by my mom. When I was five, my family moved to our Toronto apartment, but before that, we lived in a small house that had a woman living in the basement. After we moved, this woman and her family continued to sleep over Christmas Eve. After five years of being in the apartment, I finally asked my mom who this person actually was. I just thought she was the woman who used to live in our basement. It turned out, she was more than that. She was... my sister – oops. Because she was a lot older than my brothers and I and she had her own family, I had no idea. Her daughter (my niece), was born the same time we moved to the apartment, so my brothers and I grew up playing more with my sister's kids rather than our own sister. They never called me "Aunt" or my brothers "Uncle." I wasn't that oblivious. Plus, before I asked, the topic never came up and my parents just assumed I knew, but nope. Talk about a Christmas surprise – I have a sister... and I'm an aunt! That certainly helped things make more sense.

When my sister's kids were old enough, they joined my brothers and I in the kids' room Christmas Eve, which meant they also got to enjoy traditions like the jingling sleigh bells. This tradition of sleeping over continues to this day with anyone in the family who can make it. It's even expanded to be from Christmas Eve until New Years. Each person takes a day for food so no one person or family gets stuck doing that. The location has varied over the years. For instance, when my ex-husband and three boys lived in our farm house, it was great for having people over. We even had a big kids' playroom that became the adults' playroom at Christmas. We filled it with blow up mattresses and various things that made it feel more grown up than Ninja Turtles could. I don't know if it's an unwritten rule or if we are always so happy to be together, but we never bickered or had any fights... Actually that's not completely true because we'd often have pillow fights, but that's different. When we get together for Christmas we essentially get to act like kids again, which is part of the magic of Christmas: You make time to see people and you're allowed to have fun.

The one tradition that's mostly been with my kids – it's going to make us sound nuts – is every Christmas Eve day before people showed up, we'd put on our pajamas and run around the farm house. I should point out that where we lived had snow, so it wasn't like we went outside and casually enjoyed the warm sun. No, we're true Canadians. After running around the house, we'd jump into the snow – again, just in our pajamas – and make snow angels before running back into the house to get warm. Over the years a few people have joined in our craziness, but my sons loved doing this so much as kids, even now as adults, they still do it.

For the most part, I have carried on the traditions my parents started like my sons got to pick one big present to ask for from Santa and it'd be unwrapped and ready to play with Christmas morning. They didn't have an Eaton's catalogue like I did; they typically went off TV commercials, which is something today's kids don't do since most people watch TV without commercials. The one year they got a racecar track that went up the walls and then they were into Ninja Turtles and Transformers for awhile. I remember they'd pull out their new transformer from the box and without a second thought they transformed it. Then I'd ask to see it, and without a second thought... I'd be stuck. I could never transform those stupid things. But even today, my boys still have a gift from Santa under the tree. The first Christmas after my oldest son, Marty, moved out he came to me and proudly announced, "This year from Santa, I want a vacuum!" I was like, "A what? Seriously, you want a vacuum?" And as requested, Santa brought him a shiny new vacuum, unwrapped and under the tree ready to be "played" with. He thought it was the best gift ever. When he found it under the tree, he picked it up and hugged it. The next day, I ended up going to his place. Because of the set up of his front door and steps, he couldn't see if anyone was there, so I snuck up and peaked into the window and there was Marty singing in the living room while dancing with his new vacuum. In that moment, I realized he truly was his mother's son (and his girlfriend scored – a guy who loves to clean? That's the best gift any woman could ask for... minus cooking, but he could do that too – I raised my boys well).

The one tradition that remained solely my own family's happened at the official beginning of our Christmas season on December first. After putting up our main Christmas tree in the living room and before any presents were put underneath it, the whole family would lay under the unlit tree and when we were all set, we would turn it on. It was such a beautiful moment. With the tree lights glowing, looking up from under the tree, it was like being in a forest looking up at the stars. We would spend hours laying there talking and admiring the lights. It was... magic.

My boys quickly learned to love Christmas trees as much as I did and they soon had their own tree in each of their bedrooms. As they said, they didn't want Christmas to turn off after leaving the living room. Each boy got to choose the theme for the tree like my one son had a Toronto Maple Leafs tree (he has great taste in hockey teams) while my other two had music themed trees. I've always been particular about how the lights are put up, so I did that on my own, but when I finished that part, my sons would help me put up the decorations while I made sure each ornament was spaced out properly – I'm anal about my Christmas trees. I know these were their trees, but they still had to look good and not be treated with an attitude of "just get'r done" with lights thrown on the tree still in a tangled ball and ornaments put on the tree with the passion of a neutered sloth taking a nap. I have to admit, I feel a sense of pride that my sons have picked up my anal retentiveness when it comes to decorating, and every year they send me pictures of their Christmas trees and ask what I think. It's surprising what you end up passing onto your children. I'm glad they took that one; it's much better than a few other options they could have picked up.

Even after my kids grew up, I never tired of great Christmas experiences. When I met my second husband, Alex, I ended up bringing my love of Christmas to his family as well. His family is Orthodox, so they celebrate Christmas and New Year's in January – a reason to have more Christmas? Fantastic. His family always had presents, but there wasn't the same magic I had with my own family... so I had to fix that. His niece and nephew were really little, so I asked permission to have some fun with them (aka freak them out). I told them if you see Santa, the following Christmas, he'll leave you a set of bells. And these weren't just any set of bells. These were reindeer bells that came on a leather strap, and Santa would write on the back of it including the year you saw him. That Christmas I had Alex dress up as Santa and while he was leaning under the tree to make him impossible to recognize, I brought the kids just outside the room and had them peak around the corner. There, right in front of them, in all his glory was Santa... at least it was Santa's butt. It may have been the least attractive angle to see Santa, but it was still him, so that's what mattered. The two kids were so excited they vibrated. It was incredible. Despite their excitement, I kept them quiet and after a few moments, I got them to go back downstairs. I'm pretty sure they didn't sleep that night because they were too excited. In the morning they ran into the room with all the adults to tell everyone what they saw. It was fantastic... until I realized I now had to find bells on a leather strap to give to them and I couldn't find them anywhere. I mean, I went everywhere looking for those stupid bells. I should've thought out my plan a little more like how my mom bought the angel hair *before* getting us to leave out a can of pop. Fortunately, Alex and I ended up finding some bells after months of stress and frantic looking. That following year when the two kids got up Christmas morning, the first thing they did was run to the tree to look for the bells. They were even more important than their gifts. And there, glistening on the tree waiting for them, were the reindeer bells as promised with the year and a note from Santa. Just like the year before when they saw him, the joy they now showed was incredible. It was... magic. My mom would've been proud.

One of the best things about Christmas is you never know what will happen. I used to drive a city bus (jealous?) and one Christmas I started handing out song books to people who got on. I would joke with them, "Study up because there'll be a test." I ended up having a woman come on the bus who dared me to sing out loud for everyone. She said, "I'll sing one of the songs if you do it first." I wasn't going to back down from a challenge, so right then I there, without any help or background music, I started singing. I ended up liking it so much, I kept singing every day I drove the bus. It was like Forrest Gump who just started running, but I just started singing. Before I knew it, this simple act grew to having my son, Marty, join me one day with his guitar and I gave out tambourines and shakers to the bus riders as the whole bus sang for several TV stations and newspapers. From that experience I met a lady who wanted me to sing backup vocals for a country singer. At the album release party, I ended up talking to someone from a radio station who asked me to come on his show. It was for this guessing game segment that was supposed to last five minutes that turned into me being on the air all morning for the entire show. Someone from the station haphazardly quipped I should be on the radio, so I said, "Make me an offer." The next thing I knew, I was working for their morning show. That's why when I talk with young people, I like to tell them to never turn down an opportunity (unless it's for the mafia) because you never know where it'll lead (that's why you say no to the mafia – you know where that'll lead). Life is all about change; it'll never be the same. Our one challenge in life is to get good at changing and to even look forward to it because otherwise we'll miss out on some wonderful opportunities.

Eventually the radio position dissolved and being open to opportunities is how I started working where I still work, the Christmas Store in Niagara Falls – yes, the Christmas Store. My family and friends think this is amazing. A friend of mine who convinced me to be in his band (another opportunity I took) was talking to the owner of the Christmas Store and it came up that he needed someone to run it. My friend recommended me and after a quick meeting with the owner, I had my next position. I've never actually had to do a formal interview for a job because being open to opportunities always led to a position.

I love working at the Christmas Store – how could you not? Sure, I frequently get asked how I can handle the music all year round, but you don't notice it after awhile. I still love Christmas music and will enjoy it during the Christmas season, but I will say that after working in radio and now at the Christmas Store, whenever I can, I enjoy silence. Silence is pretty amazing, and it's a reminder that the simple things in life are often the best.

One of the things I love about the Christmas Store is how it naturally brings out joy in people. It won't even be Christmas and people get excited as soon as they see the store. That's the power of Christmas. It makes people feel better; it makes people *be* better. Christmas is the one time of year, people who are typically more selfish and self serving end up taking a moment to give to others. People who would normally never think to give are suddenly handing money to the guy at the side of the road or calling family they haven't talked to for a long time. Occasionally, there'll be someone who looks grumpy when his wife gets excited about the store. I'm not sure if that's because he's just a Bah Humbug kind of person or if he's thinking this is where he's spending the next three hours of his life and a large portion of the vacation budget, but I'll jokingly call him the Grinch and welcome him to the store, and all the guys end up smiling and being a little happier... at least for the first hour.

It's pretty amazing how just the thought of Christmas brings out thoughtfulness and a spirit of generosity as many people want to buy something for every special person in their lives. Working at the Christmas Store, there's nothing better than making someone's day when they find the perfect gift or something to cherish themselves like a married couple who will be celebrating their first Christmas together or grandparents who have their first grandchild. It's particularly meaningful being able to write something on the ornament that they'll get to admire every Christmas season for the rest of their lives.

The joy and generosity that Christmas brings is something I wish people did all year round, but it's like when the decorations go away, so do the heartfelt sentiments. That's one of the great things about working at the store – it helps people have that goodness come out all year round and I get to be part of that.

At my own house I have it decorated for December first. That's the way it always was growing up. I start decorating in November and by the end of the month I have a tree in every room decorated with its own theme just like when my boys were at home. The living room is the silver and gold designer tree while another room has the tree that's all about the poinsettias and the spare bedroom is all elf related with the headboards and shelves being decorated as well. My husband says I have more decorations than God... and he might be right. God probably has more pictures of his Son like a normal parent would, but I'm pretty sure I have more Santas and snowmen. From December first I get to enjoy the decorations until February first. A statement I know makes many people cringe (with jealousy). I claim it's so my Orthodox husband feels like his Christmas and New Years are properly included, but... I think you know the truth, and that'll be our little secret.

Some people would call my parents Christmas freaks (I would be one of those people), and I strive to be just like them. And with any luck, I'll be able to help there be future generations of Christmas freaks because the world could use a few more of us. Christmas is so much more than just one thing. It's everything good in our world brought together to encourage and inspire us to feel better and be better. Christmas is... magic.

Questions You can Ask to Create a Fun Christmas Conversation

The author of this book (me) is a psychotherapist, which means I'm all about engaging communication (unless I'm tired and then I'm like a zombie… my wife will attest to that). It's amazing how the right question can spark a more meaningful and connecting conversation, yet so many discussions get stuck on lame talking points. These questions will hopefully give you a starting point to have better conversations without having to think for yourself (I love not thinking for myself… my wife will also attest to that).

1. What was your favourite tradition growing up? What is it now?
2. What is the one Christmas moment you wish you could relive?
3. What is your favourite Christmas memory?
4. What is your favourite Christmas moment... a) growing up b) dating c) after marriage d) after kids e) after your kids grew up?

5. What do you think would make your Christmas this year more meaningful and/or fun?

6. What was your best Christmas gift receiving moment?

7. What was the gift you were most proud of giving?

8. What is your favourite Christmas decoration?

9. What is your favourite Christmas picture whether from your childhood or present?

10. What is the one food you want to eat to help make it feel like Christmas?

11. Is there a movie or thing you have to do for it to really feel like Christmas?

12. What helps you get in the Christmas spirit?

13. If you could be anywhere for Christmas, where would you want to be?

14. If you could have anyone at your Christmas this year, who would it be?

15. If you could have anyone who has passed away at your Christmas this year, who would it be?

16. What is the best Christmas movie besides *The Muppet Christmas Carol* (e.g. I can see *Love Actually* being a possibility)?

17. What is the best Christmas TV show episode? (e.g. *According to Jim* when he accidentally plugs his neighbor's toilet with his Santa beard and floods the bathroom or Josh Groban's Christmas episode on *Ally McBeal*)

18. What is your favourite Christmas song? Album? Singer?

19. What is the worst a) Christmas movie? b) Christmas TV show episode? c) Christmas song (e.g. Feliz Navidad)?

20. What is the worst (or funniest) Christmas experience you've had?

21. What does Christmas mean to you?

22. Is there a different season that gives you more hope or sense of joy than Christmas?

23. What's better for you: seeing the stores filling up with Christmas excitement in November, the anticipation in December, Christmas Eve, Christmas, or New Years?

24. What is the most fun you've had at Christmas?

25. If you could be friends with any Christmas movie character in real life, who would it be?

Author's Note about the Following Stories

(Yes, I have a lot of author's notes because yes, I like to ramble and make things all about me.)

The following stories range in material and subject matter because they were written for various reasons and had different inspirations. For instance, some stories are more innocent in nature while others are more grown up because they were inspired by issues I saw as a therapist or they were lessons I needed to learn and remember. Because of this, each story will have a rating above the title to help give better direction as to what to expect. That being said, my background is working with teenagers and adults, so I really have no idea what ages will find my stories appropriate. Considering my two year old loved the fire breathing dragon at Universal Studios while much older kids were scared, sometimes you really can't guess what will work and what won't. What I do promise is that I don't use profanity or include erotic novel inspired moments... and I guess using the word "erotic" makes this section PG; my apologies for not warning you, but I trust you're strong enough to survive.

For ratings, I'll use F for "Family" or PG for "Probably Grown-up."

The important thing to remember is that all of these stories were written with love and completed because I had fun writing them. Not every story is my favourite, but every story has value (even if it is just to make the book longer). It's like a parent with their children – not all of them are your favourite (can I write that?), but they all have value; a statement that definitely makes this section PG and possibly scarring for some people: (reader) "I always thought my parents loved my sister more, but now it's confirmed… this author just ruined Christmas!"

My hope is that you will be entertained, maybe learn something, and, ultimately, feel a little more Christmas-y.

Christmas
STORIES TO ENCOURAGE & INSPIRE

Why Bible characters could never see a modern-day psychologist.

The Ultimate Christmas Tree

B eing a Christmas tree is the greatest position in all of plant kingdom. These trees are groomed and manicured to be as beautiful as possible because they will be used to celebrate the most wonderful time of year. On one Christmas tree farm, there was one particular tree that grew like no other. Her name was Rose. It was an unusual name for a tree, but it helped emphasize how beautiful she was (and how thorny she could be). There was no particular reason why she was so beautiful, but there were guesses: "Perhaps she was fertilized by stardust," said some. "Perhaps her seed was planted by an angel," said others. Whatever it was, Rose was magnificent... and she knew it. Unfortunately, as with most beautiful things, Rose became obsessed with her appearance. The more people admired her, the more pressure she felt to be beautiful. On top of this, the more concerned she was with being beautiful, the more judgmental she became of others. It was a vicious cycle that left her heart cold. She was beautiful, but this became a barrier for her. Some of the woodland creatures were afraid they weren't good enough to approach Rose while others couldn't be bothered because there was nothing welcoming about her. One time, a squirrel in desperation climbed her to escape his predator, but Rose threw him from her branches because she didn't want to be damaged. Rumors quickly spread and the small creatures kept their distance. Even the birds avoided her and they're bird-brained. Rose never really noticed that she was being avoided, and even if she had, she wouldn't have really cared because she was so obsessed with looking her best. Unfortunately, she was so worried about pleasing the farmers that whenever one gave another tree attention, she would seethe with jealousy. She would say to herself, "Look at how hard I'm working and how good I look! I should be all the farmers need to be happy."

Some of the other trees had moments of feeling sorry for Rose because of her obsession with perfection, but none of them dared talk to her because she could be downright mean. Behind her back, they would talk though. Some said that "Rose smells like manure" – ew – and "Rose is a giant thorn in disguise" – ouch – and "Roses are red, but Rose is blue; she has the warmth of an icicle" – burn. (Trees aren't very good at rhyming, but you get the idea).

As the years passed, the Christmas finally came when all of the trees in Rose's field were to be cut down and shipped to the store to be sold. This was an exciting time for these trees. The day before they were to be cut down, they had a great celebration where they said good-bye to their animal and bird friends. All the trees were bursting with anticipation… except Rose. She was still busy trying to be perfect.

During the cutting down time, all of Rose's hard work for perfection seemed to pay off as she was given special treatment by the farmers. They were particularly careful not to bend any of her branches when they handled her and they even put her in a special stand all by herself. When she and her fellow trees arrived at the store, she was put out front as a way to draw in customers while the other trees were kept in the back. Everyone thought she looked so beautiful. Everyone admired her. Everyone was amazed at how perfect she was… yet no one wanted to buy her. She was beautiful, but there was something unwelcoming about her. A couple people enquired, but she was too expensive for them, so they bought a different tree instead. Each time someone chose another tree, Rose was hurt as she thought, "Why didn't they choose me? I'm much more beautiful than any of the other trees. What do I have to do to impress people enough to want me?" With each rejection, it was harder and harder for Rose's branches and needles not to droop just a little more. Hours turned into days, days turned into weeks, and soon all of the trees were bought and taken home… except for Rose. And because of time and discouragement, she was now just a glimpse of her original beauty.

When the store officially closed for Christmas Eve, Rose was the only living thing left. Even the waving Santa was turned off. She was completely alone, and it was official, no one had wanted to bring Rose home for Christmas. Her entire life was spent preparing for this experience and now she was going to be alone at Christmas. Rose was confused and in a state that was flipping between sad and angry: "I tried so hard to be the most beautiful tree anyone has seen and here I am, alone. What more could I have done?" Rose's part anger soon began to settle into full blown sadness and she began to cry and cry with tears of sap rolling down her trunk. Her needles fell and her branches drooped like wet hair.

She didn't know how long she had been in that state when a car pulled up beside her. It was an older car that was in need of a lot of love (or to be scrapped). This car looked quite the opposite of the beauty Rose once displayed. In her earlier days, she would've snubbed her nose at it and made fun of whoever drove it, but she was so desperate for company that she didn't even mind the puff of black smoke the tailpipe shot out when the car was turned off.

Soon the car door slowly opened and closed, and a woman in an outfit that matched the car appeared in front of Rose. Rose was suddenly aware of how droopy

47

her branches looked and how saggy her needles were. She was embarrassed, but there was nothing she could do. This was her – imperfect. Slowly Rose looked at the woman's face afraid to see the disappointment in her eyes because Rose was the only tree left and she didn't have much beauty to offer. Instead, the woman had tears in her eyes, and she wasn't sad. The tears were for another reason. The woman looked up and down Rose and a smile grew on her face as she whispered, "You're perfect." With that, the woman pulled a box out of her trunk and began to decorate the tree. There was a mix of ornaments. They were nothing like the fancy decorations on the trees in store displays. There were paper chains, old toys with hooks in them, and ornaments so old they were likely tossed out by people who felt their beauty was too far gone to keep. These were obviously ornaments the woman had gathered and made. They were nothing like the ones Rose imagined would be hung on her branches... yet they were beautiful. They were better than beautiful; they were… perfect. And with each ornament the woman put on the tree, Rose regained a little more strength. By the time the woman was done putting on all of the decorations, Rose had regained her original brilliance, but this time she was covered in decorations like a true Christmas tree.

In the morning, the backdoor of the car opened to reveal two young children. They had been sleeping in the car while their mom worked to set things up. The children quickly jumped out of their seats and screamed with joy when they saw the tree. It was magnificent. "Mom, Santa was here!" they cheered. Under the tree were several presents wrapped in newspaper and homemade bows. The kids bounced around and soon began to dance around the tree and sing, "Oh, Christmas tree, oh, Christmas tree..."

With heavy bags under her eyes after her long night of work, their mom emerged from the car. Rose could tell the woman was exhausted, but she was happy as she saw how excited her children were and she beamed when they hugged her. Rose had never seen anything like this before. This family clearly didn't have a lot. They lived in an old car and wore old clothes, but they were the most beautiful people Rose had ever seen. In that moment, something changed in Rose. She realized that life isn't about being *good* enough; it's about *loving* enough. Rose had missed that. This time Rose felt tears of sap slide down her trunk because she was so full of joy. This was what Rose had longed for, but didn't know how to get.

Suddenly, Rose felt a weight on her one branch... and then another... and another... and another. Then there was a strange digging into her trunk. Birds were landing on her branches. Small creatures were climbing up her trunk to sit in her foliage. Soon, Rose was bursting with creatures wanting to be close to her because she was so warm. She had never experienced this before and it felt... right. The family who was once hugging each other was now staring slack-jawed at the tree filled with birds and small creatures. They had never seen anything like that before. No one had. This truly was a magical Christmas.

Over the next few days, Rose, like many other trees, was taken down and dropped off at a park for her final resting place. As Rose lived her remaining days on her side in a field crammed with other trees, she had never been happier. She now understood what it meant to have friends, and she loved joining in on the sharing of their Christmas stories.

In the field of former Christmas trees, everyone was happy, but no tree was as happy as Rose as she was now glistening with love and joy. Birds bumped into each other in order to have a chance to rest on her branches while animals fought to use her as their home because she was so warm. Once again, Rose was the most beautiful tree in the field, but this time, her beauty was real. This time, her beauty was from her love and that made all the difference.

The end.

The Ugly Elf

Y ou might be surprised to hear that the whole "elves make toys and Santa delivers them with a sleigh and reindeer" idea hasn't happened for a very long time. This idea has been maintained, however, for marketing purposes because it sounds so magical. Unfortunately, it's just not realistic. The whole thing originally began with Santa giving a few toys he handmade to poor children in his village for Christmas. He loved doing this so much it grew to include giving presents to all the children in his village for Christmas. In order to reach even more villages, Santa brought in the elves to help make toys and he used a sleigh pulled by reindeer to move faster and cover more territory. This continued until there was a stalemate. Santa could not feasibly do any more villages in one night unless he came up with a more efficient way to distribute the toys. That's when the concept still used today was adopted. The movie *Arthur's Christmas* was close to the truth, but Santa's operations aren't that technically elaborate. Instead, there's a little more magic involved. In order to achieve global distribution in one night, the North Pole uses portals. It's not like in Star Trek where anyone or anything is "beamed" anywhere. It's more like *Monster's Inc.* with the doors to children's rooms. Instead of doors, however, Santa has elves distribute gifts through Christmas trees, poinsettias, and nativity scenes. Using these three portal options means if people don't put at least one of them out, Santa can't give them gifts. It was never meant to be exclusionary, but that was the downside of using the portals. On the plus side, it helped simplify things and not upset any parents who didn't want to participate. Years ago, there was a petition for the menorah to be included, but the Jewish leaders in charge of the agreement refused to accept Dec

25 as the official day to receive gifts because it felt like they were conforming to Christmas. The problem made sense, but unfortunately, Santa didn't have any options to offer because the portals only opened on Christmas Eve. Santa was stuck.

I should point out that like any good business, Santa had to adapt where he could. For instance, eventually plastic toys took over, which meant the elves making handmade wooden toys came to an abrupt end. Fortunately, the elves weren't laid off; they were redistributed to have two main types of jobs. This leads to another interesting point: There are two kinds of elves. There's the most known kind who are cute and adorably happy and then there are elves like Pug – the ugly ones. Pug was given his name because he had a smushy face like a pug. And no, this wasn't a nickname; this was his actual name. His parents were cheerful, but surprisingly mean.

Following the idea that there are two kinds of elves, there are also two kinds of jobs for elves. It's kind of like at a restaurant where the attractive staff members are out front while the ugly ones are in the back (no offence if you work in the kitchen). Of course, in a restaurant when someone is being hired you can't say, "Yeah, you have the face of someone who should be hidden in the back." Instead, it's more like "We need a dishwasher," or "Those hands look like they'd be good at chopping vegetables and wiping away tears for being so ugly." Similarly, the one group of elves was put into positions that involved the public like working in stores and at parades while the other elves got put in the warehouse and used for distribution. Guess which elves got which jobs?

Please know this wasn't Santa's fault, and none of the elves were upset with him because it was again out of his hands. It turns out it's bad for business when people see an ugly elf and want to throw up, which was always a risk. These elves were ugly. I mean seriously ugggggllyyyy. That's not said in a judgmental way, but in the way that someone says body odor smells bad. It's just a fact.

If the ugly elves are responsible for distribution, you probably guessed that Santa doesn't deliver the presents anymore. His job has actually become busy all year round instead of just one night. Instead of having a workshop of elves making toys, he has to oversee everything and coordinate with all the toy and electronics companies for the gifts he needs. How does he afford to outsource like this? That is still a North Pole secret. This story can't give everything away. What can be said is Santa was a great boss who was jolly but firm. He had very clear expectations and the elves did their best to be obedient because they knew it was for a greater good. Of course, that didn't mean the ugly elves never dreamed of something more. They may have accepted their lot in life, but that didn't mean they didn't aspire for something different.

The benefit of the elves distributing the gifts was they can move incredibly fast. They're so fast the human eye can't see what's happening and then suddenly the work is done. This means elves are fast enough to deliver every present between the first stroke of midnight and the last like the whole Cinderella at the ball idea. The elves have to be that fast because at the last stroke, the portals close. Out of the entire year, the portals are only open for those twelve seconds. Fortunately, the ugly elves always finished with time to spare… until one night. This story is all about the one Christmas that changed things up bigger than they had been for centuries.

Before we can get into the story, there is one last thing that needs to be known. All the ugly elves delivering presents work in pairs. Pug's partner was Rudy, and he was a stickler for rules. Many elves thought he was a jerk because he loved the rules so much. He didn't want to be mean, but rules gave him comfort and helped the world make sense. Part of him also secretly believed that if he followed the rules perfectly, he'd be good enough to move up from the ugly elf position to be with the attractive elves. That had never happened, but the ugly elves all liked to dream. Rudy's motto was "Perfection is what Christmas is about." Being such a stickler, it was hard to feel Christmas cheer around him, but there was always some because it was Christmas. Pug was very different than Rudy. His mom used to say what he lacked in looks he had double in the warmth of his heart. That can sound great, but having a warm heart can lead to a lot of hurt, especially because it's hard not to feel others' pain or take criticism too personally.

One Christmas, Pug and Rudy were doing their Christmas distribution tasks, but Pug was feeling emotionally worn out and discouraged. He felt stuck and was simply going through the motions… that is until the last house of the night. The pair should've realized something was different right away as they had trouble getting through the portal because there wasn't much of a Christmas tree. It was more like an indoor plant wrapped with some popcorn on a string and a few school-assignment-made paper decorations hanging off of it.

When Pug and Rudy were finally able to get the portal open and they were putting out the gifts, Pug heard a child crying. Because he's a sucker for tears, he went to see what was going on. Rudy lost his mind. He was screaming at Pug to get back because they were on their way to a record-speed gift distribution night. Fortunately, an elf scream is like a dog whistle except only elves can hear it.

In the next room, Pug found a young girl talking to an even younger girl.

"You need to go to bed," said the older girl. "Santa can't come if you're still awake."

"I don't care if he comes," cried the little girl.

"Don't you want a present?"

"What good is a present when Daddy is sick? He won't even be here for Christmas tomorrow!"

"I know," whispered the older girl. "Nothing really matters right now, does it? Maybe there'll be a Christmas miracle for us." When the older girl said this, it was clear she didn't believe it, but she was trying to encourage the younger one.

Being so warm-hearted, Pug was particularly heartbroken for these two young girls. He even felt guilty because a few seconds before he was sad about having a mundane life when these girls had real problems. Not sure what to do, he started to walk back towards the portal thinking about what he could do to help them. Passing a window, his eye was drawn to a for sale sign on the front lawn.

At this point, Rudy was really freaking out. Now it wasn't about making a record. He was screaming because the clock was about to chime for the twelfth time, which meant the portal would be closed until next Christmas Eve at midnight. If Pug didn't get back immediately, he would be stuck there, which would create a problem never before seen in the history of Christmas – losing an elf. Pug might be ugly, but he still mattered as much as any elf.

For the first time all night, Pug smiled a big smile and wished Rudy a Merry Christmas while waving to him. Meanwhile, Rudy said something very not merry or Christmas-y just as the portal closed. As Pug let it close, he knew what he was going to do – hence the smile. In a blink of an eye, he completely fixed up the house including repainting it, putting up new trim, and scrubbing it spotless. He figured if this family was selling the house, by fixing it up properly they'd be able to make a little more money off of it, or, if nothing else, they could feel proud about their home when others walked through it. It was seconds of work for Pug that would've been months for a human. He even had time to clean up and decorate the outside for Christmas, so others could see what a beautiful home this was.

Pug felt fantastic, better than he ever remembered feeling… but that's when it hit him. He'd been so focused on helping the girls, he forgot one major problem – he didn't have a way to get home. What was he going to do? Should he try to walk to the North Pole? That was a bit far. It'd take him at least a day, and even if he got there, what would happen? He just broke a lot of rules. He could lose his job in the ugly elf department.

He could even be banished from the North Pole… What would Santa say?

Pug didn't know how long he was stuck in his thoughts, but he suddenly heard with his very good elf hearing what sounded like something landing on the roof. He quickly hid behind the couch not sure what was going to happen. Just as he hid, there was a poof. As the sweet smelling, candy cane cloud started to dissipate, Pug could hear a familiar voice nattering on. It was Rudy. This wasn't a good sign.

"It's worse than I thought! See Santa. He didn't just miss the portal, he's also cleaned up the house and made it look incredible. How could he have done such a terrible thing?"

Pug couldn't hold himself back. His guilt and fear were too high. "I'm sorry!" Pug bellowed the words. He slowly came out from behind the couch and approached them. "I'm sorry for breaking the rules. I just couldn't help but feel sorry for the family. Their house is for sale and their dad is sick in the hospital. I know I'm not supposed to do things like this, but I had to. I needed to do something special for the girls who were in the other room crying."

"See, that's the problem. You're so worried about how it makes *you* feel, rules are ignored. You are just so selfish. Isn't he Santa?... Santa?"

Santa stood staring at Pug. It seemed like he was thinking, and then he spoke. "I remember when I first got into this. It was pretty amazing how I could bring joy to others by doing something kind. Over the years, it became so much I had to put in rules to keep it happening as smoothly as possible. There was so much going on… it was overwhelming."

"Yeah, and that's why we have rules because we need them in order to do bigger things. Rules are very, very important and you sir, ripped them up and tossed them in the wind like they mean nothing," piped in Rudy.

"Perhaps… but there is something more important than rules?" said Santa.

"Really?" Rudy was genuinely intrigued. Rules were all he had known.

"The most important thing is love," cheerfully said Santa. Since they arrived, Pug finally felt the courage to look up at Santa. "Love is more important than rules and I've lost sight of that. I've been so busy I've forgotten why I got into this in the first place. Thank you for reminding me about what is more important. It was also nice having a reason to pull out the old sleigh."

Just then, the little girl Pug had seen crying earlier came out and whispered, "Santa?"

"Well, hello little one. I hear you've been having a really rough time lately," said Santa in his jolly but sincere tone. Meanwhile, Pug and Rudy scrambled to hide behind him for fear of scaring the girl with their ugliness. "I wanted to personally do something special to encourage you." Santa started to push Pug out from behind him. "But don't thank me. Thank my very special elf here. It was his idea, and he even did all the work here fixing things up and decorating for you."

The young girl just then realized how different the house looked. She was speechless as she gazed around. Seeing her expression was really wonderful for Pug. He may have distributed presents for many years, but he had never actually seen a child's face light up when they saw the gifts.

Looking around, the young girl started to cry. When Santa asked her what was wrong she replied, "This is the most beautiful the house has ever been, but we need to sell it. We can't afford it anymore because Daddy has been so sick."

The two elves and Santa stood speechless not sure what to do. Rudy was the first to move. He slowly and cautiously moved towards the little girl who continued to cry. Carefully, he reached his hand up and placed it on her shoulder. He wasn't sure what the protocol was because this had never happened before, but he followed his instinct.

As soon as he touched the young girl's shoulder, she threw her arms around him to hug and then she cried with her face on his shoulder.

Just then, the older girl came rushing in. "Sorry Jen, I was in the bathroom. Are you okay?" And just like her sister, the older girl stopped and stared. "Santa?"

"I hear you've been having a house problem," Santa gently said.

"Uh… yeah," gently responded the girl, "but do you mean the falling apart problem or the 'we can't afford the house' problem and need to sell it?"

"Thanks to my elf here, the first problem has been addressed."

The older girl was surprised by his words, but then as she started to scan the room, she realized it wasn't how it was before. It was… perfect. "How did…? Wow…"

"And I think that maybe I should be following the example of my two elves here who have shown wonderful kindness. I may not be able to fix your dad, but I can make your situation a little better." With that, Santa reached into his bag and pulled out a piece of paper and handed it to the older girl. "Give this to your parents. That should solve the second problem." Santa then snapped his fingers and the for sale sign outside disappeared.

"I don't understand," said the older girl.

"Have you seen the black and white *Miracle on 34th Street* movie?"

"Yeah?" replied a confused young girl.

"This ending is a lot like that, but instead of a new house, you get to stay exactly where you are." The older girl, once again, just stared in amazement. "And starting this year, I'm now doing what I call a Christmas miracle moment. Every year one family will be chosen to be given something extra special, and thanks to these two elves, you were chosen this year." Pug and Rudy looked at each other as Santa whispered to them, "You're being reassigned to this new department." Turning back to the girls, Santa continued, "So if there's anyone you should thank for this, please thank them." The older girl continued to stare. Santa leaned over and whispered, "This would be a good time to say thank you to the two elves."

As quickly as the older girl had become speechless before, she snapped out of her trance and grabbed the two elves and started to hug them. After a brief moment, the younger sister joined in the hug as she asked, "What's going on?"

While grasping tightly to the two elves, the older sister sweetly replied, "We have our lives back."

After a few minutes of being in the embrace, a faint whimper could be heard coming from the group hugging. The older sister started to let go as she asked, "I'm sorry, am I hurting you?"

"No…" whispered Rudy as he started to hug everyone back. "I never knew what love and acceptance felt like before. It's… it's… beautiful."

After a few minutes of letting the elves and the girls hug, Santa announced, "Sadly, it is time for us to go. There's still a lot for us to do tonight."

As the elves said goodbye and walked towards Santa, the youngest sister ran over, grabbed both of them, and gave one last squeeze as she whispered, "Thank you for making my big sister happy… I've missed that." And as she let go, Santa and the two elves disappeared up the chimney leaving the two girls a chance to really look around at how wonderful their house now looked.

And from the roof, sleigh bells could be heard as Santa cheered, "Merry Christmas to all, and may your lives be full of love this year!"

The end

Charlie the Mall Christmas Elf

Charlie was the best Christmas elf anyone at the mall had ever seen. He was gentle and kind with a flair for making everyone laugh from little babies to grumpy dads stuck shopping for hours longer than the five minutes they could handle. This, of course, helped parents get the best possible photos of their kids (unless you prefer the photos of kids crying, which are hilarious when the kids are grown up). Charlie had been an elf for eight Christmases now, yet he was continually finding new ways to make people smile. He'd frequently use his favorite jokes and magic tricks, but he was very quick witted, so he was regularly making new jokes and learning new tricks in his off time to share with people. He was so good at his job he had the record for the mall of being given the most phone numbers by single moms (and not so single moms). Charlie was also the only employee to never get sick, which was surprising when he was the total opposite of a germaphobe. He was even quick to help the snottiest nose kids feel better. His bosses weren't sure what kept him so healthy whether it was his jolly spirit or his obsession with home remedies like his daily doses of oil of oregano and cups of water with dissolved baking soda. Either way, they loved how dependable this made him, which was on top of being the best elf at getting kids to smile for pictures. This made it particularly difficult for them to disappoint Charlie as they said no to his yearly request. You see, despite all of the praise Charlie received as an elf, every year he applied to be Santa because that was his dream since childhood.

As a young boy, there was one year when Charlie's family was struggling financially, and a man dressed as Santa randomly showed up at their front door on Christmas to give him and his sister presents they would never have even dreamed of asking for because they were such fancy gifts. Somehow, this man heard about their situation and his generosity changed Charlie's life forever.

Unfortunately, Charlie wasn't able to be a mall Santa because he was too short. This wasn't an "I'll sue you for discrimination" kind of thing; after all, the staff loved him. Instead, it was the fact that his legs were too short for kids to safely sit on his knees. It was actually a liability situation where the mall didn't want any children to get hurt. This year when Charlie applied for the Santa position he showed his bosses how he could use mannequin legs for the kids to sit on while he stood behind them like they were his own. He even made an outfit to hide what he was doing. Admittedly, it worked well, but his bosses still said no because it seemed too weird.

Charlie's short stature may have added to his brilliance as an elf, but it also added to his passion for being Santa. You see, he was always the shortest kid in his class growing up, and he fervently believed that people would only respect him if he was either taller than them or in a position of power. Since he couldn't significantly change his height and he was too kind to be a savvy

71

entrepreneur, his only option was to be in a position people admired that didn't require him to take advantage of others. Unfortunately, as joyful and accepting as Charlie was of everyone else, he struggled to accept his own shortcomings (yes, that's a pun). The only consolation for Charlie was every Christmas Day he dressed up in his own Santa outfit and gave gifts to kids in the hospital. It was the grand ending to his favorite time of year and the one time he was able to be Santa, which, in his eyes, was the one time that made him someone worth caring about.

Then one foggy Christmas Eve day, Charlie's bosses came to say, "All the Santas are too sick to work; we're messed!" The store didn't have a Santa to be in the photos for the hoards of families lined up for last minute pictures. While they panicked, Charlie grabbed his mannequin legs outfit in order to remind them how he could be Santa. His bosses were desperate, so they said yes. To their surprise, Charlie's idea worked perfectly. His legs never got sore from kids sitting on them, and by standing, he had greater leverage to help kids up onto his lap. Plus, he had a literal ankle biter and he was completely safe because it was the mannequin leg the kid was biting (and chipped a tooth on).

This was a momentous day. Charlie had done it. He was finally in the position he dreamed of having since he was a kid. He was finally someone everyone respected. People wouldn't look down on him for being short or for being just an elf. He was the mall Santa, the King of Christmas, yet... he hated it. Charlie wasn't allowed to joke and have fun like he did as an elf because there wasn't time. He'd quickly say hi and then pose for the photo. Any time he tried to joke, the management would point to a clock; he had a job to do, and being funny wasn't part of that. What made it even worse was there wasn't an elf there who could get the kids laughing like he could. The other elves had always relied on him to do all the greetings and silly things to get the kids to smile. Not only was it awful for him to see so many unhappy children, the parents were complaining that they had heard this was the best place to get the photo done because the pictures always ended up with extra happy children. Sure, people were tired and stressed with it being Christmas Eve day, but Charlie had always been able to get people laughing no matter how bad it was.

Now he was stuck watching everyone be miserable and he wasn't allowed to do anything about it. He was supposed to be the King of Christmas... yet he felt like a prisoner behind his beard and hat. He had wanted to be seen as something more than himself; he wanted to feel important and now he realized that he had been all along as an elf. After all this time he now realized he never appreciated what he had because he was too busy wishing for something else. It suddenly dawned on him that being Santa had never really been about how other people saw him because they had already appreciated him. It was actually about how he saw himself. He had been blind all of these years by his own insecurity. Being Santa was a great privilege, but Santa was only as good as his elves, and Charlie made his Santa's look amazing. He didn't need to be the King of Christmas. He just needed to appreciate himself the way he should.

Christmas Eve day dragged on for Charlie, but it eventually ended. Charlie's bosses told him he did really well, but they clearly weren't as thrilled with the day as they normally were when he was an elf. He was good as a Santa, but he was great as an elf. He knew with practice he could be really good at being Santa, but he didn't care anymore. He wanted to be where he made the biggest difference and that wasn't behind the mannequin legs that allowed him to be the mall Santa. Charlie's power came from behind the camera and he was excited to realize that he could be happy with himself for who he was. He could even be happy that he was short because that helped him be better at what made him great.

The next day, like every Christmas, Charlie went to the hospital to give presents to the sick kids, but this year instead of being Santa, he was Charlie the Christmas Elf. He made everyone smile from the crankiest baby to the most worn out parents. Charlie may not have been the "King" of Christmas, but he helped everyone there laugh and feel like life wasn't so bad, which was the greatest gift he could give. He didn't need to be in a position or power; he just needed to help others feel valued, which started with him valuing himself.

The end.

Rated F

Why Santa Gives Coal

I n a pleasant time, in a pleasant town, in a pleasant home, there was a pleasant family (this was clearly before the internet ruined the world). They were a very kind and friendly family (this was definitely before the internet). One day, the son, Johnny, asked his mom how Santa in all his goodness could leave coal for kids who were on the Naughty List; it seemed mean. His mom told him that was a very good question and then explained that Santa wasn't punishing the kids as much as he was encouraging their parents. Santa figured if the kids were on the Naughty List, they'd

76

be very frustrating to handle, and by giving the kids a gift the parents could use to heat the house, Santa was helping the parents. Plus, there was hope that this unwanted children's gift would inspire the naughty kids to behave better. Johnny was really glad his mom could help him see that Santa's actions made sense. He wanted to like Santa and this made it easier.

That following Christmas, Johnny had been dreaming of Santa bringing him a Lionel Electric Train (this was definitely before the internet), and like every child his age, he would write a letter asking for it from Santa. Actually, he wrote many letters to Santa because he was so excited at the idea of having a train with its own whistle. Fortunately for Johnny, he had been raised to always do his best to be good and to be considerate of others. He was definitely on the Nice List, so things were looking good for him.

That December, however, followed a tough season. As pleasant a town as it was, business was business, and there were layoffs at the local factory. Like many others in the town, Johnny's dad was laid off, which put his family in a scary spot financially. Suddenly, Johnny's Christmas wish seemed too selfish, and he felt like he had to do something for his parents. Normally, Johnny's parents gave him a little money to buy presents for them and his siblings as he was too young to have a job and they liked the idea of their children being thoughtful and giving to others. That year, however, he'd have to be really creative because there wouldn't be any money for him to use, which was at a time when his parents were in the most need for his thoughtfulness.

Johnny was scared for his family. He didn't know what they would do or if they'd lose their house. He was also scared because he had so badly wanted a Lionel Electric Train from Santa, but how could he receive such a wonderful gift at a time like this? Even if he was given the train, he couldn't enjoy it if he was afraid of being homeless. There must be something he could do to help his parents... and then he remembered what his mom had said: "Santa gives coal to naughty children to help the parents." That's what he could do. He could always ask for the train next year. This year he needed Santa's help to do something for his parents, and what could be better than taking away some financial stress? This idea gave him hope, but what would he do in order to get on the

Naughty List? He'd been so good that year; his naughtiness would have to be even better (so to speak).

The worst thing Johnny could think of doing was murder... but that was too far – very too far. He then thought he could have an affair; that would be bad... but that would mean he'd first have to get a girlfriend and girls had cooties. Plus, he hadn't had the proper cootie shot yet to protect himself, so that was too risky. The third option was doable – he could bully a smaller kid. The problem was he didn't want to actually hurt anyone. There needed to be a line of doing something naughty, but without it being hurtful... and that's when it hit him. He could steal something! That'd be awesome! He could rob a train like in the movies… Wait, no; a nine year old isn't going to scare grownups into giving him their money with his squeaky little voice. Then he thought he could rob a bank… Wait, no; he could get arrested or shot... or worse, he could miss school hiding from the police (Johnny was a serious geek and loved school). Johnny then had the epiphany of all epiphanies. He could steal something and then return it after Christmas. Santa wouldn't know he was going to return the item. He'd just know that he stole it, which would make him be on the

Naughty List this year and back on the Nice List next year. It was perfect.

Johnny was really excited about this idea and with Christmas only days away, he had to act fast. He decided that the safest thing for him to steal would be a bag of animal feed from his friend, Tom, who lived on a farm up the street. He would steal the extra feed they didn't need for a few weeks, so he could return it after Christmas. No one would even know it had been missing. It was perfect.

That night when everyone in Johnny's house was asleep, he snuck out of bed and out of the house to go to his friend's farm. He was always a good boy and doing something that looked so bad actually made him really excited. The best part was there wouldn't be any guilt either because he knew he'd be returning the feed in a couple of days.

To see Johnny sneaking down the street, an outsider would wonder if he had done this before. He moved stealthily and was wearing all black. He was even wearing a black toque and a black scarf to hide his face. The only thing not black was the white tag dangling off the toque.

Johnny had bought it with the plan to return it after using it, which was like a bonus naughty thing to go with his break and enter experience.

Everything was going as planned, Johnny was able to sneak into the barn where he knew the family kept the feed and no one was around. Excitedly, Johnny grabbed the bag... and that's when he realized the flaw in his plan – the bag was too heavy for him to lift. He tried dragging it, but he was just too small to move it. Fortunately, Johnny didn't panic. He had seen too many movies where the robber panics and does something really dumb that gets him in trouble. Instead, Johnny took a second to think and look around the barn. That's when he saw it – a saddle. Johnny realized this was just as good an idea because the only thing the horses might be used for at this time of year was to pull a sleigh and they didn't need a saddle for that. Johnny was proud of himself for keeping his cool and thinking through the problem. The saddle would be heavy, but he could manage. It was perfect.

As Johnny picked up the saddle, he heard a familiar but nervous voice. "Put the saddle down or I'll stab you with this pitchfork... this very dirty, poopy covered pitchfork."

Johnny quickly took off his mask and said, "Don't shoot!" He had clearly watched too many bad action movies where that's what people said.

"Johnny?" exclaimed a very surprised Tom. "What are you doing?"

Johnny couldn't lie to his friend; he wasn't that bad a kid yet. He was honest about everything. He told Tom about his dad losing his job and how he wanted to give his parents coal to help heat the house. Tom loved the idea and shared that his dad was struggling financially, too. With a smirk he said, "I want in."

"You can't steal from your own family," protested Johnny.

"Then we need to do something different," suggested Tom. "After all, you've already admitted your plan, so now Santa will know what you're doing." Johnny nodded to show he understood and then... they stared. They didn't stare at anything in particular. They just stared as they thought about what they should do. After a long pause, Tom cheered, "I got it!"

"What?" asked an excited Johnny.

"Ummm," stammered Tom. The next thing Johnny knew, he got punched in the face.

"What was that?" questioned Johnny.

"My ticket to the Naughty List," smiled Tom.

Johnny paused for a moment as he thought about this new idea, and without warning – bam! He punched Tom in the face, which caused both boys to groan.

"Punching really hurts the hand," complained Johnny.

"What about my face?" whined Tom. "Why'd you punch me so hard?"

"Sorry, I got excited," apologized Johnny. "How about no face shots?"

"Good idea," agreed Tom. "And we don't have to hit so hard that it hurts."

After a brief moment, the two boys looked at each other and then Tom hit Johnny in the shoulder. Then Johnny hit Tom in the shoulder. Looking into the other's eyes, they nodded and then started hitting back and forth. This continued as the boys got into this strange kind of game where they'd hit each other and then they'd yell things like "Did you see that Santa?" "How about that?" and "Are we on the Naughty List now?" The boys did this until they were too tired to keep hitting each other. As bruised and sore as they were, they felt fantastic. They felt accomplished having done something to deal with their fear and they had connected with each other on a whole new level. It was the kind of connection that can only happen when two people work through their pain. It was perfect.

The next day was the last day before school ended for Christmas holidays. All the kids were sad. They weren't sad that school was almost done (obviously), but they were all sad and scared about how their families were struggling financially. The tough fall season had affected everyone in some way. All the kids were gloomy... except Johnny and Tom. Later in the day, some of the kids noticed how they were the only ones happy. This led to one of them asking why they weren't sad like everyone else. The boys hesitated, but they were so proud of what they did the night before, they had to tell the small group of kids around them. Very quickly, the word got out and the entire student body was soon crowded around Johnny and Tom. They wanted to see how it worked... so the boys showed them. Johnny and Tom pointed out there were to be no face shots to limit evidence that would upset their parents and all punches needed to match in force in order to prevent anyone from feeling mistreated and limit the risk of someone getting angry. And that's when it started. Tom hit Johnny; Johnny hit Tom; and suddenly, all two hundred kids in the school were punching each other. What made this scene even stranger was the kids were soon screaming things like "Watch me Santa! I'm naughty!" and "I'm so knotty I use the improper form of 'naughty' in my outburst!" As an outsider looking in, this was hilarious (unless you were a teacher or principal at the school). It was hilarious because it was such a contrasting scene of violence and happy children; it was a fight that seemed to make the kids happier. It wasn't hilarious to the school staff, however, because they were naturally panicking about tears and possible injuries. Unfortunately for the teachers, when you have a group of kids wanting to be on the Naughty List who are having a great time punching each other, trying to stop it just means you're getting punched. In fact, the kids enjoyed punching the teachers so much they forgot the rules of not too hard and no face shots – oops.

After about fifteen minutes, the kids started to wear down and lose interest. The school staff didn't know what to do because it was such a bizarre experience having all the school children in a punching fight with a joy the teachers had never seen before. It brought even more joy than recess ever had, so that's saying a lot. Eventually, it came out that it was Johnny and Tom's plan to get on the Naughty List to help their parents. The teachers started by affirming the students they would all be on the Naughty List, but then added since there weren't any serious injuries (minus Mr. Jacobs's injury, but nobody liked him anyway), they would pretend it never happened. The entire school body was then warned that if it happened again, there'd be serious consequences for those involved.

Johnny and all his schoolmates returned to being good and obeyed this request. It helped that Johnny figured he was safely on the Naughty List as he had been sent to the principal's office for instigating the biggest school fight ever seen. He felt good knowing he had done what he could for his family and there was a sense of community that developed with his schoolmates that would keep them connected for the rest of their lives because they would always have this crazy story to talk about: "Remember that day we broke Mr. Jacobs's nose?" (Sometimes stories get exaggerated over time… but this time it didn't.)

Christmas morning, was a mix of feelings for Johnny. He woke up dreading having to explain to his parents why he was on the Naughty List, but at the same time, he was also excited to have a gift to help them. Before going to the tree, Johnny asked his parents if he could talk to them. They said that wasn't the time because he had to go see what was under the tree. He tried to tell them that that's what he needed to talk to them about when, from the other room, he heard a whistle. The train?! Johnny was shocked. His plan didn't work! How did it not work? Was Santa crazy? Johnny quickly ran into the other room and there was the train he had so wished for and beside it was a heaping pile of coal. Johnny was very confused, but there was a letter addressed to him. He quickly opened it and it read, "Dear Johnny, I love that you wanted to sacrifice your own gift in order to help your parents. That was very loving of you and very deserving of being on the Nice List. How about next time you just send a letter asking for some coal on the side? Love Santa. PS I have to say, you had all of us in the North Pole laughing at the scene of your entire school punching each other with big happy smiles on your faces and screaming at me to watch. Arguably the funniest part was seeing Mr. Jacobs get whacked a couple times. You know, he never made the Nice List? What you did is good for building community, but next time stick to sports or music."

Johnny couldn't help but smile and cry at the same time. He was proud for being able to give Santa something to laugh about and, at the same time, he couldn't be more excited to give his parents his gift (provided by Santa). He then decided to tell them what had happened because they were a little confused by the coal. After the story, and when his parents had stopped laughing, they both hugged Johnny and told him how much they loved him. They also said that it was their privilege to take care of him and they would always find a way to provide for him. He didn't have to worry. He just needed to enjoy being a kid... preferably without violence.

The end

The Good Samaritan
(Revamped)

M any years ago in a small town, a shopkeeper was busy cleaning up after a long day. It was only two days before Christmas, so business was particularly good that week. As the candles began to burn out one by one, the shopkeeper paused to enjoy the moment. He was weary but happy. He took a deep breath and smiled because he felt truly blessed. Everything in that moment was just right.

Suddenly, there was a crash and two masked men burst into the shop. The one man lunged at the shopkeeper and hit him with a club. The only thing the shopkeeper noticed before everything went dark was a tattooed crest on his attacker's arm for a group that was known to be very dangerous.

When the shopkeeper woke up, he touched his stinging head, which felt crusty from the dried blood. He slowly got up and looked around to find the place he hid the money was broken open and everything of value was gone from the shop. He then reached in his pocket and he felt the couple coins he had kept in there for emergencies. That was the only money he had left from his biggest week of the year. In a daze, the shopkeeper locked up the store and began to walk home.

It was a cold night, but the shopkeeper didn't notice because he was still in shock from the night's events. As he slowly walked down a quiet country road, he noticed just up ahead in the ditch was what looked like a person partly curled up. The man was only wearing a long shirt, which was unusual for any time but it was particularly unusual when it was so cold out. As the shopkeeper approached, he noticed beside the body was both a mask and a club. The shopkeeper hesitantly looked at the man's arm and there it was – the tattooed crest of the group. The man lying in the ditch must have been one of the robbers. This could be the very one who hit him. The shopkeeper just stared at the man who was in the ditch not moving. It looked like he was breathing, but he was badly beaten. There was a lot of blood and his arm, which should be pointed the one way, was bent in the opposite direction. This man was in serious trouble. His partner in crime must have turned on him, beat him, and made off with the money – *his* money. The shopkeeper didn't know what to do. This was the man who participated in knocking him out and stole his Christmas earnings. This man stole the money he needed to provide a Christmas for his own family. The shopkeeper wanted to take the club and have a couple swings himself. Instead, he simply said, "You're not worth it. You're not worth me even hitting you." And he started walking away. Someone else could take care of him.

After the shopkeeper walked a few minutes down the road, he looked back to give one last scowl. As he did, he noticed that another man was coming up the street. The shopkeeper recognized him; it was the town priest. As the priest approached the man in the ditch, he looked at the man, paused, and suddenly scurried across the street and continued on his way pretending he didn't see the injured man. He must have seen the tattoo on the man's arm because the shopkeeper knew how evil the priest thought the group was. Shortly behind the priest was one of the town's lawmen. When this man saw the body, he ran to it, and bent down. When he got up, he had the club in his hands, and he started swinging at the man in the ditch.

The shopkeeper was conflicted. Should he care? This criminal was getting what he deserved, but for some reason the shopkeeper found himself running back screaming at the lawman to leave the man in the ditch alone. Fortunately, the lawman obeyed and ran away like he was afraid of being identified. When the shopkeeper got to the body, he was once again alone with the man who had helped beat and rob him; he was a man rejected by the priest and a lawman who was so disgusted, he added to the beating. The shopkeeper simply stared at the man bleeding in the ditch. He touched the gash on his own head, which part of him hoped would make him remember the anger he had, but instead the shopkeeper felt sympathy. His heart filled with compassion. With all the strength he could muster in his weakened state, the shopkeeper slung the man over his shoulder and slowly began walking home repeating the words of Jesus: "Love your enemies. Pray for those who persecute you. Love your enemies. Pray for those who persecute you. Love your enemies. Pray for those who persecute you..."

The next day, the man from the ditch woke up in a strange house. He groggily asked where he was and a woman greeted him through gritted teeth who said, "The man you beat up and stole from found you in a ditch badly injured and brought you home to help you get better." The man from the ditch was confused. The woman further explained what had happened and that her injured husband found his attacker knocked out in a ditch with only a shirt on. With eyes blazing, she then stared hard at the man and said, "My husband, the man you beat and robbed, saved your life and then he used the only money he had left after you robbed him to pay for *your* doctor. That was the kind of man you stole from. That was the kind of man you knocked out and left bleeding in his shop two days before Christmas!"

The injured man was baffled. He had no idea why she was accusing him of robbing her husband. At the same time, however, he was blown away by what he heard her husband did. He would never have imagined that someone who had been beaten and robbed could show such love to his attacker. After pausing for a moment, he asked why it was assumed that he was the robber. The wife told him about the tattoo on his arm. Looking down, there it was. The injured man was even more confused. What was going on? He then asked the woman about his horse. The wife laughed and said there wasn't one and that it must be nice to be rich enough to own a horse. Anxious and in pain, the injured man blurted, "I promise you that I am not who you think I am."

The wife again laughed, "Yeah, like I'm going to believe you. Every guilty person would say that. You're just afraid of me… like you should be."

The man continued to explain that he was the king's top messenger. After the wife laughed even harder, he took a damp cloth he had by his bed and started scrubbing his arm. As he had expected, it was painted on like someone wanted to frame him. He then explained that he had been riding on a quiet road on his way home when he was ambushed by two men in masks. The last thing he remembered was a man with a tattoo on his arm hitting him on the head with a club. The wife didn't want to believe the man because she wanted to be angry. At the same time, she knew if her husband could bring him home after what happened, she could at least look into it. What'd she have to lose?

When her husband woke up and was ready, he took the man to the palace as his wife asked in order to prove the man was lying. As soon as the two arrived at the palace, the guards greeted the injured man with relief in their voices. It turned out the man from the ditch was, in fact, who he said he was. He hadn't made anything up. He actually ended up being more valuable than he had let on.

When the king found out, he was thrilled to see his messenger was safe after wondering what had happened to him. The king had the shopkeeper go home and return with his family in order to join in their Christmas celebration. While he was away, the messenger told the king the story and he was blown away at the compassion and grace that was shown. When the shopkeeper and his family arrived, they were treated like royalty and they joined in the feast to celebrate Christmas Eve, which was in a way that was beyond anything the family could have imagined. After the meal, the king presented the shopkeeper with a medal for his generosity and a gift of money that was more than double what he had lost in the robbery. The shopkeeper was severely wronged, but because he didn't give up on love, good still prevailed, and he and his family were given the experience of a lifetime.

As hard as it can be to offer love as defined as patience, kindness and self control, especially when we've been hurt, it truly is the greatest gift we can offer for the benefit of both others and ourselves. In the end, love always wins.

The end.

Steve "The Nobody" Narwhal

S teve the Narwhal was about as interesting as you'd expect of someone named Steve (no offence if your name is Steve). It was like someone had painted his entire personality and physique beige. Nothing stood out about Steve accept maybe how completely ordinary he was. Actually, there was one thing interesting about him and that was his dad – he was famous. Before Steve was born, his dad was playing ring toss with friends, and the one time he jumped up to catch a ring, he ended up snagging Santa's falling toy sack, which kept it from falling into the water. After this amazing "catch," he swam it to shore keeping it out of the water the whole way. It was an incredible scene that was a total fluke. To add to the craziness, it wasn't the real Santa's sack (the real Santa is more careful with the toys); there was a Santa movie being filmed and the fake Santa dropped the sack from his "flying" sled. The whole thing was caught on camera and the director was so excited about the footage, he made a whole other movie based on that one scene and he called it *How the Narwhal Saved Christmas*. It was a direct to TV movie, but it became an annual household favourite.

Having a famous parent wasn't as good as many would think. For instance, it continually reminded Steve of how ordinary he was and that he would never be as important as his dad. The worst was when anyone found out who his dad was because they'd flip from not caring about Steve to suddenly caring a lot insofar as they'd ask him about his dad. Steve went from being "The Nobody" to being a conduit to his more important dad. It was bad not being noticed, but it was even worse being noticed for something you had no part of and it was something you already had resentment towards. Actually, the worst part for Steve was anywhere he went with his dad, his dad would get stopped for an autograph or picture while he got brushed aside. Even if the whole family was there, they'd all end up off to the side waiting for Steve's dad as he dealt with the eager fans. It left Steve feeling like he didn't matter and he never would.

Steve was so uninteresting he came from a nuclear family with a nurturing mom and a dad who was engaged in the family life as best he could despite work and fame. Having a sister meant he didn't even have the weird only child thing happening (no offence to weird only children… hopefully your name isn't Steve). Steve really had nothing interesting about him. He even hit the average for everything from tusk size to weight and colour. He would've felt better if he had an unusually small tail, or a bizarrely shaped tusk – anything that was different. Part of Steve even wished he could get bit by a shark or nicked by a boat engine or harpoon, so he'd at least have a cool scar and story of his own.

The idea of a youngster wanting to stand out is pretty typical, but it grew to be an obsession for Steve. He desperately wanted to be a somebody. He wanted others to stop the family to greet *him* for a change. On the plus side, Steve didn't play the victim and wallow in his own sadness. He tried really hard to find something where he would stand out. He just didn't have any luck. Steve tried being a star athlete at ring-toss, hola-hooping, and fencing, but he was average at all the narwhal games. He tried dressing like a sawshark and getting on shark week, but he couldn't fool anyone since sawsharks get up to about five feet in length and he was closer to 17 feet, and sawsharks are about 18.7 pounds and he was closer to 4200 pounds – a slight difference. He learned those facts after. Steve even painted his tusk red and wrapped lights around it offering to lead other creatures through murky waters, but that was just weird. Steve couldn't get anything to help him stand out.

As always the case, before Steve knew it, it was Christmas Eve. Every year all the local ocean creatures got together to watch *How the Narwhal Saved Christmas.* It became an annual tradition as everyone liked having an excuse to see each other and the older generation liked to reminisce about how exciting it was to have a film crew in their waters. Everyone loved doing this… everyone except Steve. When the movie was starting and Steve's family was getting huddled together to watch, Steve's dad noticed he wasn't there, so he told his wife and daughter he'd be back. He found Steve where his son always went when he was upset. With the voice of a genuinely loving parent, Steve's dad enquired, "I'm guessing something is going on; want to talk?"

Steve was too embarrassed to share what was bothering him, so he just shifted away from his dad. Steve's dad continued, "It's Christmas Eve and I was hoping to spend it with my three favorite narwhals." Steve shifted again. "We can play ring toss or we can pretend we're pirates and try to steal the penguin's candy..."

"There's no point!" interrupted Steve.

"Why's that?" Steve's dad asked surprised.

"Because I'm not good at anything," Steve retorted.

"You're not good at anything?" Like a typical parent, Steve's dad was about to give a list of things to prove him wrong (that never actually helps), but fortunately, he was interrupted.

"I know I can *do* things, but what I mean is I'm not the best at anything. I'm completely average in every way! I'm... I'm... ordinary!"

Steve's dad was confused because, like any good parent, his son and daughter were his two favourite achievements. "What do you mean you're ordinary?"

"I want to be extraordinary like you!" exclaimed Steve.

"Extraordinary? I'm a narwhal who had a very lucky moment," explained Steve's dad.

"But you're famous. Everyone knows you and wants your autograph and photo."

"Yeah, I can see why the attention looks good, but it's actually pretty annoying most of the time. I never get to be normal and not have to worry about how I look or what I'm doing because I know if I say or do anything really dumb, it'll make the news and become a bigger issue."

"But everyone loves you," Steve exclaimed.

"It definitely looks that way when people stop me, but they love the idea of me; they don't actually love me." Steve's dad paused to think for a moment and then continued, "There's nothing about me that makes me better than anyone else. I'm just recognizable." To change gears, Steve's dad asked, "Do you know what I wish?" Steve was silent. "I wish I was ordinary and not have others interrupting my time with you."

"What about how excited people get when they see you?" Steve questioned.

Steve's dad grinned, "I'll be honest, every once in awhile it feels pretty good to have people excited to see me, but other times I feel embarrassed. I don't feel like I deserve all the attention. I didn't even mean to catch the sack, and when I swam it to shore, I was trying to find a way to get it off my tusk. I didn't want to dump it in the water in case there was something bad in there. Humans are always dumping their garbage in the ocean, and that's what I thought was on my tusk. I did what anyone who thought they had garbage stuck to their nose would do. Besides, if I had to choose between making strangers I may never see again excited or make my family happy, there isn't a second thought. Coming home from work to a family happy to see me is the best moment of my day because I'm happy to see you, too. Cheering fans is a great ego boost at first, but then it becomes noise because it's just another creature I'll never really know excited for a moment. Besides, if they see me again, they won't be as excited; it'll just be me again. Fame is very fleeting whereas the love of a family is real." Steve was starting to understand what his dad was telling him, and he began to feel better about who he was. Steve's dad added, "The only thing I'm always happy about is being with you and your sister... except when you were babies and cried all night. That wasn't ideal... you cried a lot." This made Steve sheepishly smile. "I hope that you can enjoy being ordinary and that your life will have some extraordinary moments like mine did. I also hope you'll never be famous because being a celebrity makes ordinary life really complicated." After Steve's dad paused and gathered his thoughts, he added, "If you ask me, you're the extraordinary one. I have never seen anyone with more drive and determination to experience new things... I certainly haven't seen a narwhal with a red tusk and lights wrapped around it. What was that supposed to be anyway?"

Steve laughed, "I had this idea that having a glowing red nose could do something special. It was pretty dumb."

"Who knows? Sometimes the seemingly dumbest looking things end up being the most inspiring," encouraged Steve's dad as he hugged Steve. After enjoying a long hug, Steve's dad asked, "Are you ready to have an ordinary night with your ordinary family that has a dad who doesn't like having garbage on his tusk?" And with that, the two left Steve's hiding spot and joined the rest of the family for a night of cheerful teasing and stealing the penguins' candy.

That Christmas Eve wasn't such an incredible experience that it would inspire a movie, but it was still incredible in its own way because Steve's dad got to have a special connecting moment with his son. There are many possible experiences we can have in life that are incredible; some are heroic and some are simple. The key is to put ourselves in places where we're more likely to experience them, which is often the case when we're with loved ones enjoying this most wonderful time of year.

The end.

Why Do People Obsess Over Christmas?

J im never understood his mom's obsession with Christmas. Every year she made a big deal of it and every major trip they did growing up she would have to buy an ornament to commemorate the event. For Jim, Christmas was really just a nuisance. It got in the way of life. He liked presents and he loved getting time off school and holiday pay at work, but it was annoying having to see extended family and do certain social obligations, especially when he'd rather be with his friends. Jim was in his last year of high school and he couldn't wait to graduate and move on. His whole world was about looking forward and nothing was going to hold him back. He was the youngest of three kids and he was jealous of how his two older siblings were already out of the house and "living life." He, on the other hand, was stuck. He was eking out any semblance of independence he could.

Jim had been swamped all first semester. He'd been so busy with school, clubs, teams, and work that he was rarely ever home except to sleep and grab some food. Jim had just started his holidays and he was home alone. It was still a few days before his brother and sister would be home from school, so it was oddly quiet. It was even quieter than usual because his mom and dad weren't home. Every night after work they would go to his grandma's house in order to clean it and get it ready to sell. It had been a tough year for his grandma and she needed to be put into a nursing home in order to be given full time care, so his parents had been busy all November and December helping her make this tough but necessary transition.

This was the first year his mom had been too busy to do any decorating, so it was less than a week until Christmas and there wasn't even a wreath on the door. Part of Jim liked it this way. It felt a little rebellious. While everyone was stressing out about nothing – because Christmas was just another day – he was relaxed and his house wasn't overflowing with unnecessary decorations. It was clean and simple just like every other day of the year.

That night, his parents called to say his grandma was taken to the hospital and they weren't sure if they'd be home for a few days. Jim took the information his usual cool self, but for some reason, later that night when he tried to sleep, he couldn't. There was something in him that wouldn't settle.

He had never been that close to his grandma. She had always been a bit hard and snappy, so he wasn't at a loss for her, but the house felt particularly empty that night. Before this, he hadn't really noticed his parents not being home because he hadn't been home either. He had been extra busy getting stuff done before school finished, so when he was home, he went straight to bed and he liked not being harassed with the typical questions like "How was your day?" "Can put your dishes in the dishwasher like a decent person?" and "Do you ever plan on cleaning your room or are you hoping to win the award for the world's messiest bedroom?" You know, questions teenage boys (and some men) find pointless.

After what felt like forever trying to sleep, something in Jim told him to get up and pull out just one box of decorations and put them out. It would be like an early Christmas present for his mom. Besides, what would one box hurt? Grabbing a box and putting up a few decorations, Jim was surprised by the sense of satisfaction he felt and how good it was to see the house become a little more festive. He'd been so used to writing papers and solving math problems for school he hadn't considered how enjoyable it could be using his hands and changing the appearance of a room. He soon had all the boxes out and he was so energized he even got started on the tree.

What surprised Jim the most decorating the tree was that each ornament brought a new memory he had long forgotten. There was the Mickey Mouse head ornament his mom bought on their trip to Disney years ago and the little outhouse ornament she bought on the disaster camping trip when it rained the whole week. There was also the ornament Jim and his brother gave to their mom for Christmas when they were really young. They did extra chores for their dad in order to earn enough money to afford it. When she opened the present, she put on such a big show… it was a great memory.

Suddenly, Jim felt a strange wetness on his cheek. He was inside the house so it couldn't have been rain or… a bird (fortunately). What was it? He wiped his cheek and realized it was a tear. He was confused by this at first, but then he realized he had never really thought about how much he cared about his family before and how much he valued his memories of them. It was easy to take them for granted just like it was easy not to think about his childhood and where he'd been because he had been so focused on where he was going. If he wasn't planning his future, he was trying to have fun in the moment with his buddies. There was always something to do that could distract him... until this moment. Putting out the decorations he was forced to reflect... and it was nice. Jim found himself putting on Christmas music and singing along as he finished the decorating. Of course, if you asked him, he'd deny it.

When all the decorations were out, Jim smiled. What he started doing for someone else became something he was doing for himself. He never understood the obsession people had with Christmas, but now he got it. Christmas was the one time of year we take a few moments to remember where we come from and the people we love. This not only feels good, it is helpful for giving us a better appreciation for where we are and guidance for where we should be going.

Whether you follow the religious aspect of Christmas or not, Christmas season helps us remember what matters to us and reminds us to care about others because it's the memories we make with them that help life be more enjoyable.

After falling asleep on the couch staring at the Christmas tree, Jim woke up when he heard a key in the front door lock. His parents were home. Without thinking, Jim got up, went to the front door, and hugged his parents when they came in the door. As his parents stood confused and looking at each other waiting to be told something terrible had happened, Jim whispered, "I never realized how lucky I was until tonight. Thank you for being my parents… Thank you for being so wonderful."

The next day Jim went to the store and found an ornament that reminded him of his parents because he wanted to commemorate the experience he had the night before. He wanted to remember the moment he realized how much he loved his family… and Christmas.

The end.

The Stressed Woman at Christmas

C arol always looked like the Queen of Christmas. She actually looked like the Queen all the time, but at Christmas she particularly stood out. She was a perfectionist through and through, but to outsiders she looked calm and completely in control. Her husband, Ron, knew better, but that's always the case when you live with someone who appears flawless – you know the truth. Everyone has bad moments – everyone. The unfortunate truth is family is often the recipient of exploding bottled up emotions, which means we should be weary of being too close to those who look perfect. Ron knew this lesson well… and couldn't do anything to fix it; he could just do whatever he could to reduce the explosions at him.

Every Christmas, Carol had the house covered inside and out with beautiful decorations. Everything she did was stunning. She had impeccable taste, especially with Christmas décor. Friends would stop by just to see how she decorated the house that year and they would lavish her with praise… if they could find her. Typically, it was Ron who did most of the welcoming because she was so busy. The biggest problem, however, was Carol's taste could be a bit pricey, which meant Ron had to do a lot of extra shifts at work to help pay for things, but he never complained… at least to her. He knew not to mess with her at this time of year. In fact, her anxiety induced behavior helped him be grateful to be at work more because that meant he couldn't be yelled at… most of the time.

One night when Ron was finishing a double shift, he received a phone call from his very panicked and angry wife screaming at him for not being at home to help her. He knew she was just anxious, but it was hard not to be upset by the way she talked to him, especially when he was exhausted from work he was doing to help *her* afford all *she* was doing. As understanding and patient as Ron could be, sometimes she got to him. On this particular occasion, she was angry he wasn't at home, but she also needed him to go to the store to pick up a few things she forgot. Part of the reason she was very angry at him was because she wouldn't have forgotten those things if she hadn't been watching the kids while he was at work. Sometimes, no matter what Ron did, he'd get in trouble. Carol was very good at spinning the blame to make everything somehow his fault.

Between being tired from work, dealing with the hurt from being yelled at, the fear of being yelled at more when he got home, and then being given a list of chores to do, Ron was feeling really anxious himself now. The second he was able to leave work, Ron darted to the store to get what was needed at home. Running through the store like a husband rushing his pregnant wife to the hospital, he was in and out like a flash and jumped back in his car to get the stuff to his wife.

Unfortunately, Ron never made it home... and that made Carol furious. She couldn't figure out why he was so late. Was he trying to punish her for expecting him to help out or was he just fluffing off her needs like some secretly alcoholic husband. While these options whirled through her mind making her angrier and angrier, she received a phone call from the hospital saying her husband was in a car accident. After getting the neighbors to watch the kids, Carol sped off to the hospital with mixed emotions. Part of her was really scared for her husband while the other part – if she was being completely honest – was angry that he was getting in the way of her preparing the perfect Christmas.

Carol's anger continued to fester and grow until she saw Ron in the hospital. For the first time she noticed how tired he looked... or maybe that was the meds. Regardless, he looked awful. He'd been cut up pretty badly in the accident and two nurses were busy pulling out what looked like bits of broken glass lodged in his face. In that moment, all concern for the perfect Christmas vanished. All the stress about anything completely vanished. Everything Carol had been worried about whether getting the perfect presents or making all the perfect goodies to share, organizing the perfect games to play, or hiring the perfect piano player and carolers to lead in the carol sing, none of that mattered now. It all seemed so small.

When Ron saw Carol, he tried to smile, but she could tell he was in pain. She slowly moved towards his bed like a dog sheepishly approaching his master after getting caught making a mess. All the anger she'd been feeling towards him was now flipped back on herself. It was all *her* fault. Ron wouldn't have been in the accident if it wasn't for her. She should never have asked him to help. She should've done it herself. In that moment she vowed to have an even better Christmas celebration than ever before, but she'd do it all herself. She wouldn't even have him work extra to pay for anything. She'd work more *and* do more at home. It was *her* problem, so it was up to *her* to make it work.

As Carol was having these thoughts, Ron said, "I'm guessing you're feeling guilty right now." She tried to deny it, but he continued, "You know what I'd like this year for Christmas?" Carol braced herself to hear him ask for that new TV he'd been wanting. After a slight pause, he said, "An imperfect Christmas." Carol was taken aback. An imperfect Christmas? He must have hit his head harder than she thought. Ron continued, "I remember as a kid, Christmas was messy and chaotic. I was never afraid of damaging a decoration and I had time to relax and enjoy the holidays. Since you've taken over the Christmas Eve parties, they have been exhausting and terribly stressful. Instead of fun, I'm terrified of getting yelled at because I usually end up being yelled at, and then after the party you spend a month complaining about how the party should've been better."

Carol wasn't sure how to respond. She hadn't been that bad... had she?

Whether it was being in a public place with witnesses or being in a hospital bed with glass lodged in his face after surviving a car accident, something made Ron braver than ever before. He continued, "I know the holidays are important to you and you want to make every year perfect, but... you make Christmas miserable."

Carol was more in shock from that comment than hearing Ron was in an accident. Even the nurses suddenly stopped pulling out glass from his face and slowly stepped away. All signs said he was about to have another "accident."

"We'll give you two a moment," said the one nurse.

"We don't want to be witnesses in court," added the other as they scurried out of the room.

Carol had always prided herself on how amazing she made Christmas. How could he say she made them miserable? She was suddenly torn between guilt and wanting to rip into him for being so hurtful.

While Carol's mind was whirling, Ron gently said, "I love you." Carol was still too in shock to respond. "I love you, but at Christmas you're mean and you hurt me a lot." Maybe it was the sincerity in his voice or the blood dripping down his face, but Carol didn't take that comment personally like she normally would. "These cuts are nothing... well, no, they hurt, they *really* hurt, but you have no idea how much it hurts me to see you so stressed on top of constantly being yelled at all December. I love you, but December is the worst. You are such a kind and generous person to everyone except me, especially at Christmas. To others you're great, but you get so worried about impressing people that this other side takes over and you're like a different person. It doesn't make any sense to me. You're so worried about impressing random strangers who don't matter while obsessing with impressing your friends who already love you. There's no one of importance whose love you don't already have, so what are you trying to earn?

This night was full of surprises. A few hours before, Carol was busy trying to get things ready for the perfect Christmas and now she was in the hospital with her worn out husband asking for an imperfect Christmas because somehow she was mean. What was happening? How could she have been so blind? Or was he just being selfish? Carol looked at her husband. Staring into his eyes, she saw the hurt and it suddenly dawned on her that she'd seen this hurt look many times before, but she just brushed it off as him being ungrateful for all she was doing. It turned out *she* was being ungrateful for all *he* was doing for her because *he* didn't enjoy the "perfect" Christmases she provided. She knew *she* didn't enjoy them, but she slaved away thinking everyone else benefited, but did they? In some way, many people must have, but the person she cared about the most didn't, so maybe she should rethink this. Maybe she should stop trying to make everyone happy and trying to prove she was worthy of their friendship. Anyone who needed her to prove she was worthy wasn't a good friend anyway. She didn't expect others to prove anything to her, so why would they expect that of her?

As always, Carol's brain was going a hundred miles a minute (or 160.934km's if you're Canadian like me), but this time it wasn't about having the perfect Christmas, it was to figure out her motives and what she should be doing in the future.

After spending most of the night with her husband at the hospital, she stopped on the way home at a grocery store to pick up a couple things for the family to have for the next couple days while she visited Ron in the hospital. While walking the aisles, she couldn't help but smile to herself. She had never really considered her husband as wise, but he really showed it tonight. He was always so passive that she didn't notice. It was really wonderful to see.

While in the grocery line, she looked at the magazine covers as many do, and the one title caught her attention: "Make this an Imperfect Christmas: Stop trying to impress your friends." Carol started laughing. Of course… but as she tried to be positive (for once), she thought wise people don't have to come up with their own wise ideas; they just need to recognize wise teachings when they're presented. Considering Ron was recovering from an accident when he was talking, he must be wise to have remembered the article. Either way, she loved her husband and he didn't need to prove anything to her just like she now realized she didn't need to prove anything to him. She just needed to accept his love and that she was already good enough. And just as she would accept that he loved her for her and that she didn't need to earn anything, she would try to do the same with her friends. She would no longer try to earn anything from them. She would no longer tell herself she needed to be perfect. Instead, she would simply be nice because being nice is the right thing to do.

This Christmas was going to be perfect in an imperfect way and it would be a time to really experience the love the season had to offer.

The end.

Another Stressed Woman at Christmas

No one in Jen's family ever really seemed to be that close to her dad, so when he passed away at the end of November, it surprised her how much of a hole it caused. She'd be the first to say that he was a good man, but he was distant. Growing up, her mom had always been her cheerleader, and now that Jen was older, her mom was more like a close friend. Jen's dad, on the other hand, if he wasn't working, he was staring at the television. He never engaged in conversation or really seemed to be that interested in the family drama. He just did his own thing. At the same time, however, if she needed anything done at her house, he was the first to help as he showed his love through action rather than kind words or affection. Her best memories of him were building things together. He had taught her some valuable skills around the house. How to carry a conversation was *not* one of them. If you asked Jen, she wouldn't know if her dad didn't engage in conversation because he was afraid of being vulnerable or if this was just some guy thing where he avoided anything emotion related. What she did know, however, was being at his funeral hit her surprisingly hard. Unfortunately, she didn't have time to address any of those feelings because she was in the middle of busy season at work and for the first time ever she was in charge of the family's big Christmas Eve party. This was a really big deal. She had never been allowed to hold Christmas because her sister, Carol, was the Queen of Christmas. For fifteen years she had held the perfect Christmas parties until last year when her husband was in a car accident right before Christmas and it led to this grand epiphany that she needed to focus on being a better person rather than the Queen. This, of course, led her to being a happier person (at least on the outside Jen told herself to downplay it). Even when Carol wasn't perfect, she was able to end up with the perfect result. In every situation, Jen felt her sister always found a way to show her up. But this year was Jen's turn. Her sister gave up the reins and Jen was going to blow people's minds… for once. All her life she felt second place to her "perfect" sister, but this year she would prove her worth and it would be so amazing her dad's absence would be forgotten and it'd be the perfectest Christmas possible.

Unlike Carol who was married, Jen was currently separated, so she was in this alone. She didn't even have her dad to ask for help like she used to, but she ignored that thought as best she could. Fortunately, work was a powerful distraction and any time she wasn't there, her time was spent gathering decorations for the party and materials to build a life-size Charlie Brown characters nativity scene for the front lawn.

After two crazy weeks of slaving away and seeing barely anything done, in desperation, Jen called her separated husband and humbly begged him for help. She promised to be nice and he could come and go as he pleased because any help would be much appreciated. He fortunately agreed and the extra help made a huge difference.

As the days continued to pass, Jen's Amazing Christmas Eve Extravaganza was actually coming together. Invitations were sent out and she had the caterers ready to feed the forty to fifty people who would be showing up. It wasn't as pristine as her sister traditionally did, but everything was more authentic to Jen's preferences. In the end, Jen was really proud of herself. She had rented an adult-sized bouncy castle and made snowmen costumes to bounce around in it that also acted like padding for bumping into each other. She brought in Zamboni snow from the local arena to spread all over the front lawn and there were three forts ready for snowball fights. She even had a petting zoo booked and invited neighbors to see it, so there'd be even more people stopping by than her sister ever had. This was going to be a truly amazing Christmas experience.

The night before it was all supposed to happen, Jen went outside to take a look at the house in all its snowy splendor. For the first time she could remember, she felt good about herself. The lights were just right and the nativity scene she built was amazing. Her husband had helped do so much for the party, but that was her baby. She did such a good job building those characters. They looked like something that should've been in a department store's display. She built and painted them exactly as her dad had taught her… and that's when it hit her. He would've been so proud of her. And for the first time since the funeral, she had a thought get past her barrier and she started to weep.

Jen's husband, who was close enough to hear her, ran to her because he was afraid something terrible had happened. Instead of seeing something stolen or broken, however, he found his wife crying for her dad. Without hesitation, he took her in his arms and he held her as she cried.

The next morning when Jen woke up, it was the big day… and all she could think about was how her dad wouldn't be there. After a month of avoiding the thought, her grief caught up to her and suddenly nothing else really mattered. Gone were her feelings of pride and excitement for showing how amazing her Christmas Eve was going to be. It was simply a day of feeling loss… and that was just the start of the day.

Before things could get started, Carol showed up to see if there was anything she could do to help. This was the first Christmas Eve she wasn't in charge and until now, she had stayed out of it, but here she was bright and early at the house before Jen could even get herself cleaned up. Jen was sure her sister was there to make sure she didn't screw up or to gloat about how much better the previous parties were, so Jen wasn't feeling particularly warm towards her sister. Add the fact that Jen was sad about her dad and this was not a good start. Fortunately, Jen had learned to fake happiness a long time ago, and after making her sister wait for a few minutes, she was able to act like the happy host. After a brief greeting, Jen even got her sister doing some work for her around the house. Shortly after, the caterer showed up, which was strange because they were extremely early. They were in a panic because in the night the power had gone off and half of the food was ruined while the rest of it needed to be cooked, but without power, they couldn't cook anything at their shop. Jen very calmly accepted the information, took a moment to gather her thoughts, and then said,

"Okay here's the plan…" While addressing the problem, in the back of her mind was the simple question: What does it matter? He won't be here.

Shortly after that, the petting zoo people arrived and Jen discovered they screwed up. Instead of the nativity animals she requested like donkeys and goats, they sent birds of prey and there wasn't time to get the right animals there. To make matters worse, Jen was terrified of birds. Once again, she very calmly accepted the information, took a moment to gather her thoughts, and then said, "Okay here's the plan…" While addressing this problem, still in the back of her mind was the simple question: What does it matter? He won't be here.

When the first group of guests arrived, they showed up with their pets dressed like nativity animals. When Jen politely asked them about it, they said the invitation said, "Come and bring a petting zoo." Jen ran off and checked the invitation and they were right. There was a typo… a typo on the invitation she had asked her husband to do. When she saw that, she continued to fake her happiness and acted like everything was the way it was supposed to be. Why not have pets there? When her husband realized what he had done, he was incredibly apologetic, but despite this setback, she seemed unfazed. Jen remained calm and told him it would work out, and while talking to him, in the back of her mind she heard the simple question: What does it matter? He won't be here.

While more guests came in with various costumed pets, sometimes real and sometimes plush, the chaos increased. To make matters worse, the caterers who were supposed to just drop off premade food, scrambled to put together some type of second-rate meal in Jen's kitchen with what they had left and could pick up from whatever store happened to be open making part of her house its own disaster zone. To add to the confusion, the caterer had misheard her and made double of what she needed, which was ultimately beneficial, but in the moment it added to the fullness of the house and the overall chaos.

As promised, many of her neighbors came by, but because of all the work she had been doing, many of those neighbors invited their own family and friends to see it. Plus, with all the commotion going on at the house, and the birds of prey flying around, even neighbors Jen didn't know came by to see what was happening (good thing there was the extra food). On top of all the people now at the house, costumed animals were running around barking and playing. Food and drinks were getting spilled, decorations were getting knocked over, and a few kids were crying because they weren't allowed to be part of the snowball fight since they were too young. Chaos reigned. With each mishap, accident, and broken something or other, Jen calmly addressed the problem while hearing in the back of her mind: What does it matter? He won't be here.

At the end of the night, when almost everyone had gone home, happy acting Jen went to her room and cried. She had held it back as well as she could, but she needed a moment before she faced the mess. When she had cleaned up her face enough to be seen again, she came out to find most of the house had been cleaned up by her husband, mom, and Carol and her family. It was the best Christmas present she could've asked for. Outside of the many drying dishes on the counter, even her kitchen was looking normal again.

Feeling a sense of relief from the house being better than she expected, Jen grabbed a bag of recycling and took it to the garage. Carol followed her without Jen realizing it, so after dumping the bag in the bin, Jen turned around to see her sister. Suddenly, Jen felt a rush of insecurity.

Carol would never have had a party get so out of hand. They were always the perfect nights with proper behavior unlike the craziness that happened that night. Jen waited to hear her sister say, "That was a disaster. I'm so happy because it makes me look that much better and proves that I should be the one doing Christmas." Instead, her sister hugged her and simply whispered, "Thank you," and started to cry.

Completely confused by this, Jen replied, "You're welcome?"

A few minutes later, Carol composed herself and let go of Jen. Without speaking, the two walked back into the house and as they stepped into the living room, everyone left at the house was standing there and started to clap and cheer. Carol joined in the clapping and stepped back to better let Jen receive the recognition she deserved.

After a few seconds of cheering, Jen's mom broke from the group in order to give her a hug. While holding her daughter, she whispered, "Thank you." This time Jen didn't have a response. She even had a hard time faking a smile because she was so confused.

As the cheering started to come to an end, Jen's mom let go and stepped away. Finally, Jen couldn't handle it anymore. She had to ask, "What is this for?"

Her mom replied quite surprised, "You don't know?"

"Know what?" Jen asked very confused.

Before anyone else could answer, Carol responded, "This was the best possible Christmas we could have had, especially this year."

Still confused, Jen protested, "What are you talking about? It was a disaster! The caterers didn't have the right food and then made too much of whatever they could muster up in *my* kitchen, the petting zoo people brought the wrong animals, and we had way more people than the house could fit while animals dressed in costumes ran around destroying everything. It was complete chaos!"

"And it was absolutely perfect!" announced Carol.

While Jen stared in disbelief at what she was hearing, Jen's mom started, "I was dreading Christmas more than anything I can remember. I just wanted to runaway and pretend it never existed, but today, for the first time since your father passed, I was able to have a few hours where I didn't miss him."

"My style of Christmas party would've caused us to spend the day crying and feeling miserable," added Carol.

"There was so much going on today, it was incredible," Carol's husband interjected.

Carol continued, "And if I was in charge of today, I would've lost my mind. I would've been screaming and ripping into people, but you kept calm throughout the entire day no matter what happened. I could never have done that! And because you were so good about it, we were all free to laugh and not walk on eggshells."

Jen's mom added, "Today is the first time I've laughed since your dad got sick!"

"If you had started yelling, I'd be either hiding or yelling right alongside you feeling terrible," confessed Carol. "Instead, you were cool and calm. You always had a simple solution and went with whatever was given to you. Your strength was phenomenal. You were such a joy to watch." And as Carol hugged Jen, she added, "I want to be more like you."

At that moment, Jen suddenly began to weep tears of relief. This time there wasn't any sadness; it was more about feeling completely vindicated and affirmed. All of the hurt she had felt and held onto over the years was now being let go; everything that she had been insecure about or resentful to her sister about, was now being erased as she held her sister. And as she cried, everyone in the room joined in the hug, several even joined in shedding tears because of how emotional it'd been since the father's death.

After a few minutes of hugging and telling each other how much they loved one another, everyone helped finish cleaning up and went on their way. The last to leave was Jen's husband. Before he left, he gave his wife a long hug, and while he held her, she said, "Thank you for reminding me why I married you. You really were incredible this month. This wouldn't have happened without you."

And with a raspy, choking back tears voice, Jen's husband whispered, "Thank you for letting me be part of this. I've missed you. I've missed living life with you." After a short pause, he added, "Maybe tomorrow we can see each other without birds flying over our heads and dogs dressed as donkeys running around our feet."

"I'd like that," Jen sheepishly grinned.

That Christmas Jen was able to realize her worth and strength. Beyond all the validation and appreciation she received, which meant so much to her, the best gift she received that Christmas was from her dad. When her dad was alive, he taught her many practical things like how to build a life-size nativity scene, but through his death, he taught her the most important lesson she'd ever learn – she was strong. Until now, she had no idea, but compared to losing him, everything else was small. As terrible as death can be, it puts life back into perspective; it helps us realize what really matters. This experience gave her a newfound sense of strength that would continue to help her be braver and more steadfast than she thought possible, which ultimately helped her be a more loving person. Some people let death make life worse, but from that day on, Jen decided to make her dad's memory a source of strength that would help her enjoy and appreciate life in an all new way; after all, she would see him again one day, so she might as well gather some good stories to share with him when she did.

The end.

Susie the Snowflake

S chool is a normal part of human life, but what many people don't realize is that there exist schools in the clouds called Cloud School (as you can tell by the name, creativity was not their strength). Unlike normal schools, Cloud School didn't have a set timeline for graduation. It changed with each class with longer or shorter gaps between graduations. Sometimes classes were bigger or smaller than others. Sometimes students were lazy and fell as rain or they were particularly mean and they fell as hail. The best classes, however, graduated as gentle snowflakes. The ultimate goal of a snowflake class was to help make a city look beautiful. Dirt and grime temporarily vanished under the beautiful white blanket as the fresh coating of snow makes everything look clean and sparkling. To achieve snowflake status, you have to be driven and hardworking, which means there's normally an underlying desire to do something big. No one had a greater desire for this than Susie. Susie was the smartest and most talented snowflake in Cloud School. Not only was she the top student, everyone liked her, which is incredibly rare for those who are the best at something. Normally snowflakes are like people and they get jealous of those at the top. In Susie's case, however, she was such a kind snowflake you couldn't help but love her. In fact, there was only one snowflake who didn't love Susie and that was... Susie. She was incredibly hard on herself and never felt good enough to be liked by others. As kind as she was to everyone else, she was equally mean to herself because she was so worried about being accepted by others and not being judged. Susie's dream was to feel good enough for her to like herself, and she believed that could only happen if she was able make a city beautiful all on her own. The fact that it was believed impossible didn't matter; she was going to do it on her own. She *needed* to do it on her own.

When the bell sounded to announce it was graduation day for Susie's class, all of the students assembled together in order to be released... all of the students gathered except for Susie because she had snuck over to the exit doors. The bell meant the doors were opened and this was the first time she was able to see the city below and it was surprisingly tiny. Susie was filled with excitement; she had worked so hard and was by far the biggest snowflake the school had ever produced. The city was so small; she'd easily be able to cover it.

Double checking to see that no one was looking, Susie took a deep breath, closed her eyes, and... jumped. She kept her eyes closed as she felt the wind on her face. It was spectacular. It was everything she dreamed it would be. After a few minutes, she confidently opened her eyes... and her excitement was instantly replaced with panic. The more she fell, the bigger the city got. In her cloud, the city looked so small, but as she got closer, she realized how big *it* was and how small *she* was.

Susie eventually landed on a tree where her fears were confirmed; she wasn't just a speck in the city, she was a speck in the tree that was a speck in the city. She thought she could do it herself, but she failed. Even worse, she could feel herself shrinking as the warmth of the tree was too much for her. Broken hearted, Susie closed her eyes again, but this time it was to cry. She didn't know how long she cried, but suddenly she felt a tap on her side. It was her classmate, Sally. Smiling, she said, "There you are. We were all looking for you at graduation. What happened?"

Unable to hide the embarrassment, Susie replied, "I... I jumped early... I know I wasn't supposed to, but I wanted to prove that I could make the world beautiful on my own."

Sally was surprised. "Why would you want to do that?"

Susie responded, "I wanted to prove myself, but instead, I learned how pathetic I am."

Sally got closer and calmly said, "That's the dumbest thing I've ever heard... This is amazing!" Susie was taken aback as Sally continued, "Finally, perfect Susie isn't perfect and screws something up. You were always the

141

best at everything. Do you know how annoying that is for everyone else, especially when you're so likeable? I always felt like a failure compared to you." Susie was incredibly confused. She made people feel bad? How? She was just trying to prove herself. While Susie was thinking, Sally continued, "Don't worry; I eventually got over my inadequacy feelings because I realized whether you're the best or not doesn't matter. We all need each other to reach our full potential – you needed me to be your best and I needed you." Susie looked around. Sally was right. The city was now covered in a beautiful white blanket. It didn't matter how good or bad anyone was at being a snowflake, as long as the class worked together, they were able to make the city beautiful. Sally paused as if she was letting this thought settle in before she continued. "You're a snowflake; you're one of a billion, and that's a wonderful thing. You don't have to prove anything to anyone; you just need to do your part and enjoy connecting with others as you do it."

Susie continued to look around and realized that it's never really been about her. She was just a speck among many other specks, and she suddenly felt a weight lift off her back. She was the best at everything in her class except for the two things that really mattered: liking herself and working with others. If she hadn't spent so much time worrying about being the best, she could have enjoyed her schooling more. She started to feel guilty for how wrong she'd been living when Sally interrupted her thoughts. "And in case you're now beating yourself up for not seeing this sooner, remember that the past is great for teaching us lessons for how to be better *now*. There's no point living in regret. Right now you should simply enjoy all the beauty that is around you. Every moment you're alive might be the best moment you're ever going to have the rest of your life, so look for the good in it and try to enjoy it." And with that final thought, Susie and Sally looked out across the city and enjoyed how beautiful it looked, and they felt proud to be part of a community who were able to make the city so beautiful even for just a moment.

The end.

The Return

T his was it. Tom had run away from home twelve years earlier, but it was Christmas and he was finally ready to return home to see his family. Tom came from the stereotypical family with two parents and two kids. Tom liked his older sister, Rachel, but he couldn't stand how perfect she was. She was that annoying sibling who always had the best marks in school and excelled at everything she tried. She set the bar so high Tom never stood a chance. Over these twelve years away, he never messaged Rachel directly, but he'd follow her Facebook and Instagram posts. She was, of course, a doctor now and doing all that entailed while raising a family. Having the perfect sister was the worst. He really wished she had been more of a screw up, so he wouldn't have looked so bad. Growing up, she always showed him up, so Tom just stopped trying. What was the point? Mom and Dad were always going to be a little disappointed with him, so why not just make life as easy as possible to endure being the family failure?

These were the thoughts going through Tom's head as he sat on the plane home. He felt a mix of dread and excitement like the feeling you get jumping out of a plane for the first time. He was excited to see his mom who was always very gentle and kind. He occasionally mailed her letters to let her know he was still alive. He knew his running would be hard on her, but he had to leave. Before his grand exodus, he knew it was a matter of time before he left, but because he knew it would crush his mom, he had delayed it as long as he could. He loved her very much, but eventually a man has to find his own way, especially when there was a dad like his. Ugh, his dad. Tom struggled not to get bitter. The last time he had seen his dad there was a lot of screaming. Tom and his dad had always had a strained relationship to put it mildly. He wasn't sure if they were just too similar to get along or if his dad was simply a jerk, but either way, they constantly butted heads.

After that last big fight, Tom left and never looked back. He was going to make his own way. He was going to live the way he wanted without that constant nagging voice of his dad judging him; that voice that was constantly telling him that he was making a mistake. Tom had heard that so often it was like *he* was the mistake. For the past twelve years, Tom had been pursuing his career in comedy. It started slow, but it had really started to pick up. He was constantly flying around doing shows, opening for some bigger named comics while getting some of his own shows with good crowds. He had a regular podcast and his manager was struggling to fit all the demands for him into his schedule. Tom had done it. He had made a career in the field he had dreamed of doing. Any time he got discouraged, he would think of his dad and those judging eyes, and he would push through. Tom could now go home with his head held high. He already had his speech prepared. He was going to look his dad in the eyes and say, "You never believed in me. You just thought I was a screw up. But I've made a name for myself. I am more than good enough to be your son. If you're not proud of me now, that's on you." Man that speech got him pumped up. It filled him with a sense of justice and power. He was finally not the screw up.

When Tom arrived at his parent's old house, his sense of power quickly vanished. He stood on the sidewalk looking at his old home unable to move. He wasn't sure how long he stood there, but he soon saw his mom frantically waving from the big bay window. He had never seen her so happy... at least with anything *he* had done. She seemed to be as frozen as he was, but unlike Tom, she had this huge smile and frantic hand wave like a kid seeing Santa. Tom didn't have much of a chance to soak in this feeling because he was jarred aware by the banging of the front door against the wall of the house. While his mom waved, his dad burst out of the house and ran towards him. He didn't even have his shoes on, which was strange because it was so cold there was snow on the ground. Tom's natural response was to recoil like he was about to be punched, but the punch never came. Instead, Tom felt his dad's arms around him and tears were now soaking his cheeks while his dad said, "My son... my son... you're home." Tom was speechless. Tom's well rehearsed words erased from his mind as his dad repeated, "My son... my son... you're home." Tom stood more frozen than before. His dad just kept repeating between sobs, "My son... my son... you're home." When Tom was finally able to move, his dad wouldn't let him as his dad kept him tightly in his arms. Eventually his dad seemed to notice that Tom was getting a little squeamish, so he loosened his grip and, with his head bowed, stammered, "I want you to know that I've been working really hard and trying to be a better person. I volunteer at a camp and I donate as much money as I can to the club you used to be part of. I've been working really hard..."

Tom, completely confused, demanded, "Dad, why are you telling me this? I haven't seen you in twelve years and this is what you're saying?"

Tom's dad took a step back, and with a shaking voice said, "I'm sorry... I'm sorry... I've been practicing what I should say and I want you to think that I'm good enough for you. I just want you to think that you can be proud of me when I was such a screw up as a dad."

Tom was now even more confused. "What? Why are you worried about *me* being proud of *you*? You're my dad. I'm worried about *you* being proud of *me*."

Tom's dad paused, "You're my son... I've always been proud of you. From the first time you were in my arms, I was proud of you. You never had to earn that."

Tom interrupted, "But nothing I did was good enough!"

With a gentleness Tom had never seen in his dad before, his dad replied, "I've always been proud of you; I was just worried about you living the best life possible. That's where I come in. I didn't know how to help you, and nothing I tried made you happy. I was so frustrated with myself at not knowing how to better help you. I felt like a failure as a dad... I just wanted to be good enough for you."

With that, Tom broke down and cried tears that had been sitting under the surface for as many years as he could remember. All of the anger was now being released through his sobs. Tom's success didn't make his dad love him anymore than before because he already loved him as much as he could. His dad just wanted to help him and didn't know how. While Tom was worried about being good enough for his dad, his dad had been worried about being good enough for him. All the while, Tom had always looked up to his dad, and similarly, his dad had always been proud of him. All of this time, both of them had been trying to earn something that was already there. How different their lives could've looked if they had simply accepted the other person's love. How different their lives could've looked if they didn't worry about earning love and simply embraced each other. Fortunately, there was still plenty of time for them to have the relationship they both longed to have. Now that they understood where the other person was coming from, their relationship had room to grow to what it could've always been.

The end.

Maggie the Manger

Everyone liked Maggie and that made sense. She was always friendly and had a knack to make others feel better by just being around her. Of course, it helped that Maggie was a manger, so her job was to feed the animals. Maggie was more than just a feeding trough, however, because she was so warm and welcoming. The animals loved having her in their stable. Part of the reason Maggie was so good at her job was because she really liked it. She liked how the animals would get excited when it was feeding time. She liked how their whiskers would tickle her sides when they ate out of her. She liked how their tongues were so warm and soft and she'd occasionally feel them graze against her. At least she normally liked this. For some reason the ruler of the land had demanded a census be taken, which brought many visitors to Maggie's little town of Bethlehem. The stable had been packed with animals for awhile now and she never got a break. It was a constant stream of give, give, give. She liked giving, but there reaches a point when you start to feel used and worn out if you don't get a break. When this happens, the things you once liked aren't as enjoyable as before. For instance, she no longer liked seeing the animals excited when it was feeding time because it was constantly feeding time for someone. She no longer liked it when their whiskers brushed against her. She no longer found they tickled her; instead, she found it annoying. She no longer enjoyed the animals' tongues grazing against her. In fact, it made her shudder how often she'd been licked by random animals she didn't even know. Maggie was able to still be friendly with everyone, but now it was more forced. She was simply worn out. The animals were generally very polite and grateful, but

Maggie needed something more. She needed something that would help her feel like she mattered in the bigger picture; something that gave her greater purpose to make the exhaustion worth it.

The last couple days were particularly hard for Maggie because her little town was so busy a young couple was now staying in her stable. To add to this, the woman appeared to be pregnant and she was now looking like she was ready to give birth. Maggie had seen a lot of births in her day, but it was always with animals and never humans. She quickly learned she didn't like human births. Maggie kept thinking to herself, "Can you please keep it down? Stop screaming and complaining about the pain; horses never do, and their babies are much bigger. Suck it up!"

Eventually, the woman gave birth, and the screaming stopped. The screaming, however, was replaced with crying from the baby. "What is wrong with humans?" thought Maggie. "Does the screaming and crying ever stop?" She was glad she was a manger in a stable and not something in the house where she'd be exposed to nonstop human interaction. Animals were so much more mentally developed. Humans were just annoying.

While the baby continued to cry, the man whose name was Moseph (names have been changed in order to protect the child) put straw in Maggie. He then covered it with a blanket. "Wait, what's going on?" thought Maggie. It was as if he was making her into a bed. "You're not putting that baby in me are you? I am a place for eating; not holding a baby. He better have a good diaper on because I don't want any messy business. Saliva from the animals is bad enough. I don't want to start being a toilet as well. That's definitely unsanitary!" After a few minutes, the baby settled and the woman named Jary (Again, the names have been changed for the child's protection) started to lean over to place the baby in Maggie. Maggie braced herself. "Ew, ew, ew, a baby…" but suddenly, everything stopped. Maggie's complaints stopped. Maggie's fears stopped. Maggie's thoughts stopped. Something was different. There was something special about this baby. He radiated peace and joy. He made Maggie feel better. Having this baby in her made Maggie feel better. She wasn't feeling 100 percent, but she was better. Maggie then realized that she was given the gift she had been wanting. It wasn't what she had expected. It didn't come without its sacrifices, but it was everything for which she had hoped. Maggie realized she was more than just a feeding trough for animals – she had true value. That day Maggie received the best gift of all. She received baby Jee-thooth (again, name changed). And to top it off, being baptized by his lack of a proper absorbent diaper wasn't as bad as she feared; it was actually warm and a little refreshing. Once again, she was able to laugh and not take things so personally. Being nice wasn't as forced as she found a new sense of value. That day, Maggie was renewed with a stronger sense of love and joy that helped her feel like the loving manger others always saw her as being. It was no longer a show; it was real, which made Maggie all the happier.

The end... or, I guess it's now the beginning.

Christmas is a Reminder

Tom was 35 years old, so he was at that weird in-between age where he was no longer a young adult and physically past his prime while not yet in the prime of his career like those in their mid to late forties tend to be. He'd been married for almost ten years, so he was in the routine of marriage and his kids were old enough for being a dad to be familiar while still young enough to need a fair bit of his attention. Overall, life was good, but there wasn't any... magic. Throughout the year he was fine with just being in routine, but Christmas was different. It was the one time of year he wanted more. Growing up he loved the music and lights, but he missed feeling the magic of Christmas he used to feel. Even as a teenager and into his twenties, Christmas was special. Singing the songs and going to parties were fun, but they were all a prelude to the big day – Christmas. Now that he was older, Christmas was... well, disappointing. Singing the songs and going to parties (if he was even invited to any) were the only thing fun about it now because Christmas day was just... busy. It wasn't fun anymore; it was chaos. He wouldn't admit it to anyone for fear of sounding petty, but he missed enjoying Christmas.

When Tom was a kid, there was nothing better than Christmas morning; it was truly magical. He always woke up early all excited to start the day, but it'd be so early he'd have to wait until his parents were ready to get up. While he waited, he'd play with his older brother until it was time to leave their shared bedroom. Then, when it was a reasonable hour, along with his brother and sister, Tom would run downstairs to see the tree surrounded by presents, which was one of the most exciting things a kid can see. The rule was they couldn't touch the presents until after breakfast, but they could open their stockings at the breakfast table. After a moment to enjoy the Christmas excitement, the three kids would grab their stockings and bring them upstairs to open in front of their parents. Tom loved this part of the day. Opening the stockings was the best part because they were like the opening act to the day. Now was the time of anticipation of Christmas turning into reality. It was like how the first part of a vacation is always the best because it's filled with hope and wonder of what is to come. At least, that's how vacations used to be. Being a kid, lots of things were exciting and new. Now? Ehn. They were a lot of work and money. Tom wasn't sure if he was too tired to bother being excited with things or if he'd done so much in his life that there was nothing new enough to get him excited. Or maybe he had just become too much of a curmudgeon.

Like all normal families, Tom and his brother and sister grew up, got married, and had kids of their own. Seeing his kids excited was good, but it wasn't the same, especially since they weren't so little anymore. Part of the problem was any excitement he saw reminded him of what he didn't have any more. Plus, it was hard to enjoy it when you were so tired. Even worse, kids nowadays seem so spoiled, which makes getting them excited feel so much harder than he remembered at their age. There also weren't the same kinds of little things to give each other like he had as a kid because of technology. Growing up, Tom's favorite gifts were things like CDs and movies, especially when it was something they could watch together on Christmas Day. Giving a gift card for a new APP or restaurant wasn't fun. Even shopping for gift cards wasn't fun… or was that him being a curmudgeon? Maybe this was all part of getting old and seeing his childhood as the good old days, but it left him pretty down.

If Tom was honest, what he really missed was spending the day with his brother and sister doing nothing. They were always such a busy family with jobs, school work, and household projects, but Christmas Day was the one day everyone in the family put everything aside and just sat with each other. Tom loved Christmas Day because he was forced to be with his family. Now, it was different, especially with the fight to get people to turn off their devices and just be with each other. Tom always wanted a bigger extended family, but as it grew, so too did the distance between everyone. Having a bigger family was fun, but he missed feeling connected to his brother and sister the way he once did.

After all the Christmas fan-fair was done and things were settling down, Tom's brother asked him and his sister to come with him to the other room because he had something for them. This was strange because they had stopped giving gifts years before since they all had too much stuff already. At least that's what was said. The real problem was they didn't know each other as well as they naturally did when they lived together and shared family meals every day. After they left home and the connection naturally dwindled, any gift felt forced.

In the new room, away from spouses and kids, Tom's brother passed his two siblings similar shaped gifts. Tom's brother was never a very emotional person. Depending on one's perspective, he usually came across as stoic or guarded. When he handed them the packages, Tom could tell that his brother had wrapped them himself. His wife definitely didn't help. She was a perfectionist and would be embarrassed to see the loose corners and uneven lines, but to Tom, the gift looked perfect. It was just like when they were kids and they gave each other gifts. It brought him back to his childhood and a time he felt wonder and joy.

When Tom opened it, he saw that it was a DVD with the title "Family Memories." His brother had made a video montage of their family pictures and videos growing up. Tom's brother sheepishly looked at Tom and sister and said, "I miss you. I miss Christmas Day when we'd be stuck hanging out with each other all day playing games and watching terrible Christmas movies. I love my family and it'd be sad if we were still doing what we did as kids, but I miss you and wanted you to know that."

Tom remained silent, mostly from the shock. His sister was the first to break the silence. "I miss you, too." And then she hugged her brother. While Tom's brother and sister hugged, Tom stood off to the side not moving. When his brother and sister stopped hugging, Tom still stood off to the side not moving…and it was becoming a bit awkward. Tom's sister and brother stared at him, but still, Tom didn't move. "Are you okay?" his sister asked.

After some more awkward silence, Tom's sister and brother looked at each other and started to leave when Tom suddenly blurted, "I hate Christmas Day!" His brother and sister turned back confused. "There's no magic in it anymore," he continued. "I love my family, but it's all just so exhausting. You two helped make the day wonderful. I miss you. I miss feeling like I know you. I've felt alone for so long. You're what's missing in my life. Thank you for this. It means a lot." As Tom finished speaking (or to get him to stop speaking) his brother and sister hugged him as a few tears were shared.

That night, the three siblings agreed they needed to make time to regularly see each other, so every third month they would spend three hours just the three of them doing anything they decided to do whether watch a movie, play a game, or complain and make fun of life together. It was all about being together like when they were kids on Christmas.

Sometimes the magic of Christmas Day isn't about the day itself, but rather it is a reminder of what we've had and wish for, so we can try to fix that for the upcoming year.

The end.

Roy the Toy

A story inspired by Samaritan's Purse

Roy was a toy in a shipment of thousands of other toy Roys. Unlike the other Roys, however, his security tab came loose bringing him to life while he was still securely strapped inside his box. Unfortunately, it was so dark in there that even when he opened his eyes nothing changed. It was just black. As he had hours upon hours of time alone with his thoughts, he started wondering if anyone else was out there. Was he the only one? What was the point of existence if there wasn't a chance to do anything more than be in darkness. It was almost cruel.

It was pretty common for Roy to feel like he was bouncing around and to hear motors and muffled beeping noises. He would imagine the beeps were a secret code between the creatures studying him in this bizarre experiment (his intelligence was so high because he was a very well programmed toy... and this is completely made up). One day, however, Roy heard a strange cutting noise and he was flipped upside down, shaken, and then his box dropped with a light thud on the ground. When he opened his eyes, for the first time he saw something other than darkness. Being able to see caused a mix of excitement and fear, but as his eyes adjusted to this new experience, he looked all around him to try to figure out what was going on.

Within minutes, Roy was scooped up and put on a shelf. Looking around, he was in a room full of shelves with groupings of toys strapped in boxes just like him, but none of them seemed to be alive like he was. After looking down to check himself out, he found a convex security mirror nearby that helped him see himself and his surroundings better. It was strange seeing himself for the first time, and in the reflection, he saw he was surrounded by many other Roy toys, but they weren't alive like he was. Despite this, he immediately felt relief. He wasn't the only one. He wasn't alone... but then he started thinking that he may not be alone, but he also wasn't unique. He was exactly the same as every other Roy. He was nothing special.

In his wrapping with nothing to do but think, Roy began to feel the weight of a new philosophical question: What's the point? If life is the same for every one of these toys, is there any reason to exist? If there's nothing special about him, why should he bother doing anything? The reality was if he was the same as every Roy, he would never be the best at anything. He would never do anything special or significant. He was just a number, which made his life feel pretty much useless.

Eventually Roy's thoughts were interrupted as he was carried to a new room. This was a much nicer area with more flash and excitement. This place was hopping with people. Many were grabbing toys; some were purchased and taken away in bags while others were left haphazardly throughout the store, which led to a disgruntled employee putting them back where they belonged. The grouchy workers would smile at shoppers and then mutter to themselves about how much they hated messy customers and how great it'd be to go to their homes to mess their places up so they'd have to clean it.

Soon the crowds dissipated and all the main lights were turned off. The room had a peacefulness to it. As Roy enjoyed the calm, a little creature with a skinny tail was scavenging around, darting back and forth like he was looking for something. Roy was able to get his attention and the mouse was surprised that he was alive. The two started chatting and really connected. They spent the whole night talking with a lot of it being the mouse explaining how things worked. The mouse even told Roy about Christmas and what a toy's purpose was. When Roy complained about it, the mouse countered that his own purpose was to try to stay alive as long as he could before being eaten by another animal. Roy agreed that a mouse's life was worse and it made him think that all of life was pointless.

Soon the mouse had to leave because the lights came back on and the room started to fill with people again. Roy never saw his mouse friend again as someone soon picked him off the shelf and bought him. Part of Roy was excited because maybe he'd get to see that there is a point to life now that he was purchased. Just as he got his hopes up, however, he was shoved in a bag and it was dark again. While in the bag, he thought about his mouse friend and whether making friends was worth the time when he would never see the mouse again. What's the point of putting in the energy to make friends if you're only connected for short period?

Eventually Roy was pulled out of the dark bag, his box was opened, and he was unstrapped. Again, he let himself be excited for what would happen… and then regretted it. Once released from his box, Roy was then put into an even smaller box that didn't have any clear plastic to see through. He wasn't strapped in anymore, but he couldn't see anything. Life was really just terrible no matter where he ended up.

While waiting for the next disappointing experience, Roy recalled something the mouse had said. He talked about Christmas morning when a child opened a present and screamed with delight at the toy he was given. Maybe there was still hope for something special to happen. As pessimistic as Roy was, there was a small part that allowed himself to dream something incredible could happen out of all this.

One day in the darkness of the box, Roy heard a human voice. It was muffled, but it sounded like someone said, "Merry Christmas. We're giving this one box as a gift to you today as a way to show that Jesus loves you. He hasn't forgotten you even though it can feel that way sometimes." Shortly after that, Roy could feel himself being passed around. As always, he started to feel hope rise up inside of him. This was it. This was Christmas! As soon as he started to feel excited, he told himself not to get his hopes up because he was always being disappointed and why would this be any different?

Suddenly, Roy was no longer being passed. His box was opened and the light spilled in. He closed his eyes and held his breath hoping and wishing to hear a boy screaming with delight... but there wasn't a scream. Actually, Roy could hear lots of children screaming with delight, but they were in the distance. Since nothing seemed to be happening, Roy opened his eyes to see what was going on.

As Roy assumed, there wasn't a boy looking down on him screaming in delight. There wasn't even a boy. It was a girl, and she just stared at him.

Roy panicked. Oh no, he must have been given to the wrong child. Why was he given to a girl when he was a boy's toy? Everything he feared was coming true. Life was not only pointless, it was cruel. How could this happen to him?

As Roy's panic had his mind whirling, he happened to look at the girl who remained silent. Looking more closely, he noticed that she just stared at him. He wondered if something was particularly wrong with him. Was he defective? Great, not only was he given to the wrong gender, he was a failure as a product.

Amidst his self deprecation, Roy noticed something about the girl's eyes. They were glossy. He started to look even closer. A tear formed and started going down her cheek. He wanted to tell himself that he must have ruined her special day, but something about her face didn't say sadness. It was more like… joy.

Slowly the girl put the gift box down and very carefully reached out and picked up Roy, holding him at arm's length in order to continue looking at him. As several more tears fell down her cheeks, Roy really didn't know what was going on, which meant he didn't know how to feel... except anxiousness.

Suddenly, the girl brought him to her chest and hugged him like when you see a loved one you haven't seen for a long time at Heathrow Airport (yes, that's a *Love Actually* reference). This was the first time anyone had really held Roy before and he liked it. He really liked it. It was so good it made all of his questions and doubt about the goodness of life go away. Being hugged made life worthwhile. This was the moment he had dreamed about and it... it... was amazing. This may be what other toys feel. It may not be unique or special; he may not be better or worse than any other toy, but this moment made everything worth it. He hadn't known what joy was until now and it was beautiful.

As the young girl held him close to her heart, Roy closed his eyes and just soaked in the moment – this absolutely wonderful and perfect moment. This was the kind of moment that made all the hurt and rejection in the past worth it.

From that day on, Roy did his best to remember that moment as a way to fight the negative voice that tried to make him doubt his existence and value. As long as he could help someone feel loved, he had a reason to continue being the best toy he could be.

There is joy in being just another number because as long as you're doing your role, you are making the world a better place, especially when doing your part leads to special moments like these.

The end.

The Importance of Being Nice

I f you didn't know, Elf on the Shelf isn't real. I'm sorry if being told that ruined your day. That being said, the concept isn't far from the truth.

This has been one of the North Pole's best kept secrets, but it's time recognition was given where it's deserved. For too long many have been serving without proper appreciation being given. Clearing this up will also correct a risky myth: Santa doesn't directly know when you are sleeping and when you are awake; he doesn't even directly know if you've been bad or good. That's not to say you shouldn't be good for goodness sake, but Santa's not creepy. He's not a fortune teller or able to read people's minds. He doesn't have access to people's computer cameras or phones to track anyone like the government. Instead, he has an army of trained informants who go around keeping tabs on all the children. No, this is not the job of an elf. That'd be way too obvious. Besides, elves already receive plenty of recognition for their work. These informants are so good they have even managed to avoid being associated to Christmas. They've been that covert. What's funny is as soon as I tell you who the informants are, you'll be like "That makes total sense!" because they've always been around. They've been brilliant as Santa's informants because they've been under everyone's noses the whole time. And who are these ninja like workers? Gnomes. Yes, gnomes. See? That makes total sense.

Ever notice how gnomes are everywhere? Yet, no one actually ever buys a gnome. No one is that weird. Even people who enjoy mayo won't buy a gnome (and they're the weirdest people in the world; ketchup is where it's at). Instead, gnomes just randomly show up in gardens and shelves. They pretend to be statues, so no one realizes that they're real, but they are very much alive, and they are in constant communication with Santa and his workshop to say who has been naughty and nice.

Gnomes have been doing this job for centuries and there was never a hiccup until one gnome put the whole program into jeopardy. This particular gnome, Gnick (silent "g"… it's gnome thing), had been following this one boy, Rik (no "c" because his parents were "different," which is their word; others would say they were "weird" – they like mayo). Gnick noticed that over the five years since Rik was born things had been getting steadily worse at home. Gnomes are typically really good at being objective and not messing with family dynamics because that isn't their job, but this particular boy stood out to Gnick. Gnick was aware he had an unusual attachment and he had asked for a transfer, but he was told to deal with it. Perhaps the boy reminded him of his own son who had grown up and moved away many years before or maybe it was because Gnick had been doing the job for so long that he had become tired of seeing good kids suffer and end up becoming jerks themselves when they got older because no one helped them. Whatever the reason, something snapped in Gnick. This snapping wasn't a total build up and explode like passive people tend to do. Instead, Gnick had started blurring the lines for several months and then one day, it was clearly not a blurring, but a blatant disregard for the code of not meddling in humans' lives.

When Ric was born, his parents were still a rather normal couple. They had the odd fight, but fighting quickly became a regular routine after his birth. Having a baby can cause a divide between a couple and this was a good example of that. Ric's mom felt that his dad didn't do enough while Ric's dad felt that she didn't appreciate all that he was doing. As far as yelling goes, his mom did most of that, but every once in awhile his dad would completely lose it and yell back even louder escalating the conflict to a major event. At an early age, Ric took to hiding under his bed whenever his mom started screaming because he didn't know how far it would go.

One night, Rik's mom's screaming was particularly bad, and when Rik ran to his room and crawled under his bed, Gnick just happened to be there frozen like a statue. Rik seemed to really like having Gnick there for company and he started talking to Gnick like he was a real person: "Don't be scared. We'll be okay. Mommy is just tired."

Gnick knew being under the bed when the yelling started was blurring the lines of what gnomes were allowed to do, but he couldn't help it. He had to do something for this poor child who was terrified and hiding. He also couldn't help that after the first couple meet ups, he just happened to always be wearing a cloth sack filled with Smarties he'd let fall out for Rik, which always put a temporary smile on the scared boy's face. And when Rik closed his eyes to try to sleep, Gnick would just happen to whisper, "You're not alone. I will protect you."

Soon the amount Rik's mom yelled increased while the actual fights between the parents became less frequent. His dad had started coming home later from work, which made Rik's mom angrier, and as soon as he walked in the door she unleashed a rant she'd been building up while waiting for him. Instead of engaging in a fight, however, Rik's dad would essentially tune her out. He'd either go to the bathroom and close the door on her or sit in front of the TV and stare at it while she rattled on. Neither one seemed to get that they were making it worse for themselves; they just continued doing the same thing day after day with it becoming a little worse than the day before.

One night Rik's mom started screaming at his dad, when Rik ran into his room to hide, in his rush, he didn't make sure the door latched shut behind him allowing the door to drift open enough for Gnick to see what was happening from under the bed. Unlike the recent fights, Rik's dad finally lost it with all the fury someone bottling up their feelings can have and he started yelling back in a rage. Rik's mom, having forgotten what it was like to be yelled at, matched his rage since he dared to yell at her when she was clearly the victim (at least in her mind). Suddenly, her hand was whipping through the air and landed on Rik's dad's face. It was hard to say who was more surprised by this, Rik's mom or dad, but his dad quickly left the hall and the front door could be heard slamming shut. No amount of Smarties could've helped Rik. He spent the whole night huddled under his bed crying and holding Gnick.

As terrible as that fight was for the couple, it became a more frequent event over the next week. Out of her desperation, Rik's mom would hit his dad and then he'd leave the house for awhile while Rik's mom cried in the other room.

After a week of these fights and watching Rik get increasingly scared and sad, Gnick finally snapped. Unlike Rik's dad, he snapped in a way that led him to pursue change. After another one of their extreme fights, while Rik had his eyes closed pretending he was somewhere else, Gnick snuck out from under the bed and went to the other room where Rik's mom was crying. With the deepest, most intimidating voice Gnick could muster (gnomes have never been known for being intimidating), he said, "What's wrong with you?" Rik's mom seemed to pause, but didn't lift her head, so he repeated himself, "I said what's wrong with you?"

While lifting her head to look around, she asked confused, "Who's there?"

"Who's there?" Gnick repeated surprised because he just realized what he was doing. After an awkward moment of silence, Gnick moved behind a large vase and responded, "I'm your guardian angel."

"No, really," Rik's mom muttered, "who's there?"

"I am your guardian angel," Gnick repeated this time with more conviction. "I am here to help you."

"Why can't I see you?" she snapped.

"Uh…" Gnick paused to think. "Because humans can't see angels. We are too beautiful for your eyes."

"Well, if you're here to help me, you're a little late on that. Where were you six years ago when I met Tim? He ruined my life!" she bellowed.

"So you think this is all Tim's fault?" questioned Gnick confused.

"Of course! I knew I should never have married him. If you're my guardian angel, why didn't you stop me?" she demanded.

"So you think the main problem is Tim is a jerk you should never have married?" Gnick was trying to wrap his head around what he was hearing.

"Yes! Why is that so hard to believe?" she demanded.

"Because that's not actually the problem," answered Gnick.

"Then what *is* the problem?" she further demanded.

"The main problem is… you're mean," Gnick replied with hesitation.

"What?" she questioned with rising anger.

"You're mean," repeated Gnick.

"Tim's the one who works longer hours than he should and is never home," she complained.

"Yeah, he does that because you're mean," reiterated Gnick.

"When he does come home, he never listens to me or even touches me," she explained.

"Yeah, because you're mean," repeated Gnick.

"He never does anything around the house," she added.

"Because anything he does gets criticized and redone… because you're mean," restated Gnick.

"He yells at me," she whined.

"Yes, he does yell at you. You're right, but that's after you've been yelling at him and he snaps. And why does he snap? Because you're mean," reframed Gnick.

"Why do you keep saying that?" she exclaimed.

"Because you're mean and you don't seem to be getting it," replied Gnick.

"But I'm not mean!" she announced.

"Does a nice person hit other people?" asked Gnick.

"But he doesn't listen!" she defended.

"Does a nice person hit other people?" repeated Gnick.

"I've never hit anyone else!" she further defended.

"Does a nice person hit other people?" repeated Gnick.

"If I'm mean, it's his fault!" she snapped.

"Does a nice person hit other people?" repeated Gnick.

"What kind of guardian angel are you?" she exclaimed.

"An honest one. Now answer me. Does a nice person hit other people?" pushed Gnick.

Rik's mom paused to gather her thoughts. "How can you say it's all my fault?"

"Did I say it's all your fault?" gently asked Gnick.

"You're implying it," she explained.

"You mean, you're assuming I'm saying it's all your fault?" gently corrected Gnick.

"What else could it be?" she asked exasperated.

"If there's a fight, the fault is shared equally. It takes two people to have a fight. For instance, how he acts fuels your behaviour – that's his fault – and how you act fuels his behavior – that's your fault. What I'm trying to say is this…" Gnick paused for dramatic effect. "You need to take responsibility for your own actions." Again, Gnick paused to make sure his point could be heard. "Let me ask you, if someone greeted you when you came home from work with an eye roll or yelling, would you want to hug the person?"

"No," she conceded.

"If, when you try to do something, your partner tells you what you did was wrong and then berates you for it for the next five years, will you want to do anything in the future?" asked Gnick.

"I guess not," she agreed hesitantly.

"If your partner yelled at you almost every day, would you want to come home early from work or engage in a conversation when it'll likely lead to a fight?" asked Gnick.

Rik's mom was starting to get really uncomfortable. "But he's a jerk!"

"Yea, he is, but did you start dating him and stay with him because he's a jerk?"

"No," she replied with defeat in her voice.

"Did he date you because you were mean?" asked Gnick.

"No," she answered even more defeated.

"So if you changed to be mean, can you be upset that he changed to be a jerk when you both became worse?" asked Gnick.

"But it's different… somehow… I don't know." Rik's mom was really struggling to find a leg to stand on.

"If you're mean and he's a jerk, is only one of you a victim or both of you?" pushed Gnick.

"But I'm just so hurt!" she exclaimed.

"And if I was talking to him, would he say the same thing, that he was just so hurt?" Not sure what to say, Rik's mom started crying. "I'll make you a deal, if you can be nice to him every day for one month and if he isn't a better husband by the end, I will personally make him suffer in any way you choose. But this means you will apologize for yelling and hitting him and then spend the rest of the month giving him appreciation and praise for anything he does. If, at the end of the month, he is nicer to you, you'll continue working at being nice."

"You want me to be nice to *him* after all he's done to me?" she questioned.

"You want him to be nicer to you after all *you've* done to him." Not sure how to respond, Rik's mom remained silent. "I can't make him change, but I can help you. I'm *your* guardian angel. I will help you this month to be nicer." Gnick paused. "You're not alone. I will protect you."

Later that night, under Gnick's guidance, Rik's mom left a note on the counter apologizing for her actions and a promise to do her best not to yell at him for one month. She also added that he was welcome to sleep in the bed if he wanted and not the couch. When Rik's dad got home, he chose to stay on the couch for fear the letter was a trick, and for the first week he was extra cautious around her. No matter how he acted, however, with Gnick's help, Rik's mom remained true to her word and she remained nice. And every day she put a note in his lunch that started, "My favorite thing about you today is…"

The night of the fight, Gnick also pointed out to Rik's mom that Rik was hiding under the bed. She had been so wrapped up in her own hurt and self pity that she never noticed he did this. Without Gnick's prompting, she immediately went to apologize, and the next day she spent time with him making a fort that he could use if he ever felt scared in the future. It was the first time in a long time Rik had been able to have fun with his mom and he really liked it. Rik's mom also really enjoyed it and made it a habit to spend quality time with him every day. This became the time where she refused to let herself be angry about anything or feel sorry for herself. This was her escape and she simply enjoyed reveling in Rik's innocence and wonder. She had been so busy feeling sorry for herself she had forgotten how wonderful Rik was.

By the second week of Rik's mom being nice, Rik's dad was starting to trust this new behavior and even seemed to enjoy it. By the third week, however, he started acting out like he was testing her niceness. Fortunately with Gnick's help, Rik's mom never lost her cool. Instead, she would firmly ask something like "To clarify, are you trying to make me angry like this is some type of a test or am I misreading it?" The really amazing thing was Rik's mom needed Gnick's help less and less. She was able to get into the routine of being nice but firm. She was never a pushover or let Rik's dad be too mean to her. She'd even excuse herself for ten minutes if it looked like things could get heated. Every time Rik's mom kept her cool, asked a clarifying question, or excused herself, Rik's dad would stare at her in amazement. "Who was this woman?" he seemed to be asking himself. By the fourth week, the couple was starting to spend time together and even laughed. Everything seemed to be coming together incredibly well until the end of the month when Rik's dad exploded, "Why are you being so nice?"

Being nice had become more natural for Rik's mom, so she calmly responded, "I know if I'm mean to you, you'll likely be mean to me, but if I'm nice to you, there's a chance you'll be nice to me. Plus, I'm trying to be the wife you married and deserve."

"Where did this come from?" he asked bewildered.

"Let's just say I had help from my guardian angel. Out of curiosity, are you angry at me for being nice or am I misreading this?" Rik's mom questioned.

"Why do you have to be so nice? You're making this so much harder!" he bellowed

"What is it?" Rik's mom gently asked.

"Gah!... I..." Rik's dad started pacing and flailing. "I... I..." Suddenly, he stopped flailing, turned, and announced with frustration, "I've found someone else!"

"What?" Shocked by this response, Rik's mom turned away, back again, and then quickly ran away slamming the bedroom door behind her. She had just enough self control to run out of the room. Any longer and she would've lost it on him like she used to do.

Rik's dad went to the door and started speaking through it so she could hear. "I didn't mean to find someone. It just happened. You and I were miserable for so long...

and… this last month has been great… and terrible because I was all geared up to leave after the last fight, but then you apologized and you were this nice person again. I kept waiting for you to be mean, so I could breakup, but you never were… and… this is really hard for me… I'm sorry." Dejected, Rik's dad left the house. Unlike the last time he did this, he left with hesitation and much regret because of his own shame. This time it wasn't to get away from a mean person or because of anger, which made it incredibly hard on him (deservedly so).

After he left, Rik's mom started yelling, "Where are you? Where are you my so-called guardian angel? Is this what you meant to happen? Was this all a cruel joke?"

For the first time in a month, Rik's mom's guardian angel didn't answer. She started to wonder if she was going crazy. She paced back and forth for a few minutes and then she started punching the bed like she'd been taught by Gnick. She continued punching the bed with all her might for several minutes until the hitting started to slow down and become weaker and slower. As the anger was replaced with tiredness, she started to weep on her bed. After a month of things seemingly getting better because of how hard she was working, she felt more rejected and alone than ever before.

Curled up on the bed with her legs dangling off it, Rik's mom was crying so hard she didn't notice the door slowly open. She was crying so hard she didn't hear the little footsteps getting closer to her at the bed. She was crying so hard she didn't realize she wasn't alone until she felt a small head and hand on her knee. She was too emotionally worn out to be startled. Instead, she slowly lifted her head and saw her five year old son now standing beside her holding a random gnome figure in his arms. When she looked at Rik, he gently removed a cloth sack that the gnome had around his neck and he lifted it towards her. Following his lead, Rik's mom reached out and received the small sack. She had never seen this gnome before and had never seen a ceramic gnome holding a cloth sack, so out of curiosity she opened the ties that held it together and looked inside. She was surprised to see it had a small handful of Smarties in it. Not sure what to do, she just stared at the small sack in her hands until Rik reached into it and picked out a Smartie. Then, with all the love a small child can offer, he reached up and put the Smartie into her mouth like he was teaching her how to eat. Rik's mom started to chew the Smartie and Rik gave a sheepish grin. Figuring she knew what to do with the rest of the Smarties, Rik took a step back and wrapped his one free arm around her leg dangling off the bed. As she took a second Smartie, Rik whispered, "You're not alone. I will protect you."

It suddenly occurred to her that this was the first time her son had ever come into her room while she was crying. As painful and scary as being without her husband would be, she wasn't really alone and that was because she had stopped feeling sorry for herself and lashing out. By being nice and doing her role as a mom this month, she may have still lost her husband, but she had gained the trust of her son. Looking at her son hold her leg, she smiled to herself. She had forgotten how good it felt to know she'd been a good person even if it was just for a month. She could hold her head high because she had stopped being so mean.

Shifting her body in order to sit on the floor with her son, Rik's mom sniffled and then asked, "And who is this little guy?"

Very proudly, Rik replied, "This is my guardian angel. He was always there when I was scared and alone under my bed. He would always be waiting for me and after I had a couple Smarties, he would whisper, "You're not alone. I will protect you." Suddenly, it dawned on Rik's mom where she had heard that before as he continued, "And now he'll protect both of us." And as he said that, Rik's mom could've sworn she saw the gnome wink at her.

After taking her son in her arms, Rik's mom looked at the gnome and said "Thank you for taking such good care of my son and helping me realize the importance of being nice." Then she leaned in and whispered, "And I know what I want you to do in order to fulfill the promise you made to me last month if I was nice and he wasn't."

This time she knew she saw the gnome wink at her and she started to laugh. Not because of the idea of vengeance, but because for the first time in a long time she realized she had regained a sense of power. She may have just spent time screaming and punching her bed, but that wasn't out of weakness. Instead, it was a sign of how strong she was. Attacking someone in the moment is easy; self control to get alone to let out the natural emotion takes great strength and because she was able to

191

demonstrate how much she had, she proved to herself how strong she really was. She may have been rejected, but she knew she would be okay. She had her self control, her loving son, and a family guardian angel with a pack of Smarties.

The End.

Blessing:

This Christmas, may you find ways to be blessed and to bless those around you as you experience love in an incredible way.

Why the best Bible stories happened long ago - even God doesn't want to deal with red tape.

Do

you have

an <u>idea</u> for a

Christmas story or

an inspiring Christmas

<u>memory</u> or <u>tradition</u> (like

what Rita shared in the forward)

you'd like included in a future book?

Please make submissions you'd like to share with the

author in case they can be used in a future Christmas

book to his website:

www.ChadDavid.ca.

Made in the USA
Columbia, SC
15 August 2021